BAHUVIDHA

THE KALEIDOSCOPE OF LIFE

A SHORT STORY COLLECTION

PAVAN KUMAR PARIMI

INDIA • SINGAPORE • MALAYSIA

ISBN
Paperback 979-8-89556-977-1
Hardcase 979-8-89588-930-5

To Amma, Ammamma and Chiranjeevi

If Bahuvidha is a Visual.

Thanks to Ms. Madhavi P

CONTENTS

Preface: Bahuvidha – The Kaleidoscope of Life *vii*

1. Break Ke Baad 1
2. Maha Subba 4
3. Samay Samay 11
4. Wish I Could....... 17
5. At The Turn of........... 21
6. Thin Line Between L & D 24
7. Gulaab Jamun Friends 27
8. My World Around... 30
9. Your Dreams are Mine.... 32
10. The Son of a Man 41
11. I am Always There with You... 45
12. In Their Shoes 50
13. To Chichu with Love 54
14. The Story Untold – Part I 59
15. The Story Untold – Part II 64
16. There is Always a First Time 70
17. That Night....... 74
18. Beyond Borders 78
19. The Last Meet 82
20. Anything But Tea 87
21. The Invite 92
22. The Gate Across the Road – Part I 96

23. The Gate Across the Road – Part II 102

24. My F*****R 113

25. The Cycle 120

26. The Story of XX & XY 124

27. And so we Move on with Love………….. 127

28. The Lucky Loaf 133

29. An Encounter with God! 139

30. Evil God with a Scarred Face! 143

PREFACE:
BAHUVIDHA – THE KALEIDOSCOPE OF LIFE

Welcome to Bahuvidha, a collection of stories that have lived in my mind, brewed over countless 3 AM thoughts, and simmered in the rich conversations I've had with life. Initially, I thought of calling this book The 3 AM Tales—fitting, since most of these ideas showed up at ungodly hours. But then, Bahuvidha—meaning "many ways"—felt like the perfect homage to this collection. These stories are layered, diverse, and unapologetically real, much like life itself.

Expect to be jolted, stirred, and served a platter of thoughts to chew on. Each story is a conversation in itself—about life, love, death, betrayal, sacrifice, and innocence. The characters? They're people you've met—some from your own neighborhood, some from those fleeting interactions that stay with you. And, more often than not, you'll find women at the heart of these narratives, holding the story's pulse.

You might not agree with how some stories end. And that's okay. That's the beauty of storytelling—we're allowed to agree to disagree, right? Bahuvidha doesn't promise tidy conclusions, but it does promise honest, heartfelt narratives. So, dive in, celebrate the complexity of life, and let's share in these many ways of seeing the world together.

Phew, my first book is finally out, and I think the happiest one on this planet right now is my heart—and maybe my mind (though they're usually at war). It's like living in my own War of the Worlds—wondering when I'll stop writing stories in my head and start turning them into reality. But here we are!

First off, a massive shoutout to my amazing wife, Jaya Sudha, and my boys, the Spi-Brothers—Spidey and Spikey. Thanks for putting up with my daily dose of madness and adventure. You let me be my quirky, restless self, and that's no small feat!

A special thanks to the one and only Chiranjeevi, who unknowingly powered my childhood. His energy shaped the superhero inside me, pushing me through life's challenges (pun intended) with one epic scene in Challenge. In fact, that scene inspired the name of my consulting firm—De Zero Stories. Talk about cinematic influence!

To my ammamma, for feeding me both love and mythology with every delicious goru muddalu. And to all my friends from school, college, and the corporate grind, thanks for tolerating my "Eureka!" moments—I owe you all a coffee (or two).

Lastly, to my parents, who left too soon. Wherever you've been reincarnated, I hope you're having a blast. This one's for you too.

BREAK KE BAAD

"Now this is our most favorite joint," Nidhin said, looking at Ramjee Panwaale. His voice held a hint of nostalgia, a bittersweet echo of happier times.

"Weird, isn't it? We've had our lights all the time and then end up here," Asha replied, a flicker of sadness dancing in her eyes.

"Sachi bolo... our first meet... our sight was a smoking session. You came for matches," Nidhin laughed, but the mirth was tinged with a touch of melancholy.

"But I never smoked in my life till then," Asha said, her voice soft. "I started faking by the time I became Guru of Dua." Her words were a testament to the lengths they had gone to for each other.

Nidhin pulled her close and kissed her, their lips a desperate attempt to recapture the passion that had once consumed them.

"Besharam ho... public hain..." Asha pushed him away, her voice a mixture of embarrassment and longing.

"Look, I did my count. We had more cigarettes than those kisses in our entire life," Nidhin said with a statistician's face. "Is it so?" Asha asked, her voice barely a whisper. "So either way, we would have damaged this society, hain na?" She winked at him, a ghost of their old playful banter.

They started walking on the beachside towards a busy crowd on either side of the road. Nidhin held her tightly as they crossed the road toward the crowd, their bodies pressed together in a silent plea for comfort.

"Give us space, dude... Give us space, dude... After all, we are the celebrities," Nidhin shouted at the crowd, a desperate attempt to assert their control over their chaotic world.

"Stop acting weird. Tumhara celebrity ka bhooth ab tak utara nahi kya? Bhooth pe celebrity ka Bhooth... LMAO," Asha hit him on his butt as they got into the crowd and started walking toward the front of it, their laughter a hollow echo of their former joy.

"When was our break-up date?" Nidhin asked, his voice filled with a mix of sadness and anger.

"You are such a bad planner, Nidhin," Asha started tickling him, her laughter forced and strained. "All in the world, you had to select this place for our break-up dinner. Now you know how expensive that was."

"To the top of it, we haven't ordered anything," Nidhin giggled, trying to lighten the mood, but his heart wasn't in it.

"Stop it, will you?" Asha moved away from Nidhin and stepped forward near the wall. She spotted many photographs hanging on the wall, with flowers on the floor.

"Did you find it, Dora?" Nidhin whispered, his voice filled with hope.

"Yeah, yeah there we are," Asha spotted their photographs on the top left, her eyes welling up with tears.

"Shit, how they don't have our pic together. Two different pics. Huh! So, they declared broke-up and dead, haa?" Nidhin mockingly shouted, but the anger in his voice was real and raw.

Asha ran towards him and kissed him on the lips, their bodies trembling with the intensity of their emotions. They stood there in silence for the next few moments while the crowd kept candles and flowers near the photographs. Some were silent. Some were in tears. Overall, there was a burden of sadness in their eyes.

"Gotta go, baby," Nidhin moved away from her, holding her hand and starting to walk away from the crowd. His voice was a hoarse whisper, filled with pain and regret.

"Why? Naya posting mil Gaya kya?" Asha questioned, her voice filled with a mixture of disbelief and resignation.

"Haa, tomorrow morning at 4:45 AM, Leelavati Hospital. This time Nidhin will be Nidhi," Nidhin mimicked in a female voice, a cruel parody of his future self.

"Suits you. By the way, you were never John Abraham, even when you are Nidhin," Asha smiled, a bittersweet attempt to find humor in their tragic situation.

"I haven't heard the news so far. But soon I hope. But I gonna miss you..." Asha stopped, hiding her face in her hands, her sobs muffled by her trembling.

"I should have never hurt your feelings. I am sorry for everything." Nidhin's voice was filled with genuine remorse.

There was silence in response.

Asha lifted her head to look at Nidhin. He was already gone, a solitary figure walking away from her into the darkness.

A smile disappeared from her face. Her eyes were blank as she looked into thin air and turned her head toward the Taj Hotel and the crowd remembering the lost souls of the terror attack. Asha started looking at her photograph and Nidhin's on the wall.

"You are right, Nidhin. It should have been one, and the date it should not have been November 26th, 2008," Asha closed her eyes, her heart heavy with the weight of her loss.

MAHA SUBBA

"Sa..." A voice trailed off from Maha Lakshmi's throat. She cleared her throat and said, "Subba Lakshmi!" rushing towards her friend from the platform to the waiting room. Maha Lakshmi grabbed Subba Lakshmi's arms, shaking her out of her prayer mode. Subba opened her eyes to see Maha pushing her against the wall.

"Are you crazy?!" Maha shouted loudly, then turned around to check if anyone was watching. She took a deep breath.

"Hey Rama! Subba, I told you to be careful! This is not the safest place. God can wait for our prayers. We need to survive first."

Subba, looking into Maha's eyes, fluttered her eyelids like a butterfly and pointed at the water pots.

"Maha, when you get angry, you look like Maha Kali!" She stuck out her tongue and mimicked the goddess.

Maha burst into laughter. "Look! You know how exactly to tease me."

"Eight years in school with you, My Maha. How can I forget our mischievous times? The only two girls in a class of forty boys, we dominated them all like Maha Kali and Maha Shakti," Subba hopped onto the nearest bench.

"Do you remember Gadhadhar? The thin and tall Brahmin boy we used to tease by touching his head?" Maha's eyes widened as she reached for a guava from her bag.

"How could I forget, Maha?" she laughed. "He used to run home for a head bath whenever we touched him. One day, we touched him ten times. Poor guy, he caught a cold from all the showers."

"Those were the days, Subba! Everything changed when you got married and left me," Maha sighed.

Subba looked at her with tears in her eyes. She wanted to cry, but she held herself back in public.

Just then, Maha was about to say something when the sound of the arriving train alerted everyone on the platform, including Maha and Subba.

"Quick, let's get on the train. We've been waiting for hours and can't afford to miss it."

"Run! Run! Run!" they both raced towards the train. Maha grabbed the door handle, jumped in, and reached out to Subba, who was still struggling to push through the crowd.

The train was slowing down on the platform. Subba stepped into the doorway. With huge relief, they both walked into the compartment, but it was packed full. Subba turned to Maha. "Looks like another journey on the floor."

But Maha had a plan. Without telling Subba, they both went to the other side of the entrance, placed a cloth on the surface, and sat down.

The train started with a screech.

"You have to be really careful for the next eighteen hours, Subba!" Maha whispered in her ear.

Even in the heavy noise, the word "careful" struck Subba's ear, and her face turned pale.

"They're everywhere, and I'm sure they might be on this train searching for people like you. You have to be very careful. All my lessons on how to survive will be useful now. Remember, all my efforts will be worth it if you can get out of here safely," Maha explained to Subba.

"Sure, Maha. Why don't you get some rest? Lean on my shoulder. You haven't slept in seventy-two hours."

"Seventy-two? No, my dear, it's ninety-six hours," Maha rested her head on Subba's shoulder, closed her eyes, and fell asleep immediately.

Petting Maha's hair, Subba started looking around. The train was crowded with people—families, young, old, chatting with each other. A few constables were sitting in a corner, talking among themselves and occasionally glancing at her.

She slowly turned her head towards the line of trees that were quickly disappearing behind the moving train.

"My happiest days were with you, Maha. Until the day I got married at twelve. I remember the day when you almost fought with my father and grandfather to let me stay for four more years so we both could finish school. I remember how you ran after the train when I was leaving with my so-called husband for my in-laws in Calcutta." Subba started talking to herself in a low voice.

"My father visited me the next year and told me that you got married too but also had the opportunity to finish school. I was sure you would become a doctor soon."

"My life turned upside down soon after the marriage. It wasn't a fairyland anymore. Soon after the marriage, they pressured their son for an heir. My respected husband is an obedient son to the world, but in the bedroom, I witnessed his true beastly nature every night."

"He used to beat me, in the name of pleasure. That happened for months."

"I tried to write letters to my father, but I would always find them in the dustbin outside my house. Later, I found out that the postmaster was a great friend to my husband."

"My father-in-law is a great leader of the community. He hardly has time for the family."

"Years passed like that. Just after the fourth year of my struggle called marriage, when my in-laws realized I couldn't give them grandchildren, they got their new daughter-in-law into the house. After that, my life turned even worse. I became the official servant for my husband and her. I had to wash her clothes and change the mattress of their bedroom after their nightly activities."

"I thought I would die someday without seeing my parents. Just then, my parents came to visit me. I kept a smiling face in front of my in-laws and my husband, pretending I was very happy there. I managed to find a moment to talk to my dad and mom while I was working in the garden."

"I literally fell down at my parents' feet, begging them to take me away. My father almost had a heart attack seeing my poor condition."

"Beti, I'm sorry, but we can't take you back like that. It would ruin our family's reputation. You have to forgive us."

I expected this response from my parents. They were both struggling for a bigger cause. My life was nothing compared to theirs.

"At least can you do this for me?" I begged my father.

"Can you ensure that a letter I give you reaches Maha Lakshmi without fail?" I requested.

They silently nodded.

Two days later, when they were about to leave, they said, "the coming months are crucial for us. There will be a new dawn soon, but at the same time, there will be clouds of chaos that will loom over us. So be careful."

"I was oblivious to everything. I was hoping that this letter would reach you at any cost. I only knew that you were living in the same city. I knew you got married, but I also knew that once you read my letter, you would come for me."

Three months passed. Not a day went by that I didn't wait for your arrival. At the same time, the city was preparing for something big—a new dawn, but also the unseen carnage of riots. Riots broke out everywhere. It was life for life.

My in-laws' house was the gathering place for all meetings. Too many guests throughout the day, and I was the only servant for them.

In the midst of the madness, when I was losing hope, I saw you at the doorstep.

There was a certain unpleasantness in my in-laws' and my husband's eyes when they saw an uninvited guest.

My mother-in-law warned me that I had only two more days. On the third morning, I had to leave.

But that same night, when the clock struck twelve, you woke me up. "Are you ready to come with me?"

I had been waiting for this question for years. I said, "Yes."

"We have a train that starts at 2:30 in the morning to Durgapur. From there, we'll wait for two days for a train that goes to Visakhapatnam. It's not an easy journey. There are risks everywhere. You have to listen to me and follow my instructions."

"I have to live my life, Maha. Just take me out of here." I cried at your feet.

"The next seventy-two hours will be a journey of life and death. I forgot my actual name."

"At Durgapur Railway Station, when a mob surrounded us, your training gave me a lifeline. They asked me to recite the Gayatri Mantra. I recited the Gayatri Mantra, Lakshmi Ashtotram, Bhagavad Gita sloka without stopping. At that moment, I knew that any mistake on my part could have led to my death. But the confidence you instilled in me saved me, Maha."

Subba's train of thought was interrupted by tears that fell down on Maha's face.

Maha woke up, looked at Subba, and looked around, yawning.

"Maha, I was so selfish. I didn't ask you what's happening with your life. I'm so sorry."

"Don't worry about me. You'll be feeling emotional. But if you want to listen, I got married a year after you. I finished my schooling and started pursuing my dream career as a doctor. My in-laws and my husband were very supportive. Just then, a tragedy struck our family. My husband died in a road accident. His last words in the hospital were, 'Don't stop pursuing your dreams.'"

"From then on, for my in-laws, they had two children—me and my one-year-old child. All they wanted was for me to become a doctor and start a hospital in my husband's name."

Subba was puzzled. Before her mood could turn to depression, Maha said, "Now eat this banana. We have to wait until tomorrow evening to cross this state. Until then, be careful."

"There was a commotion around when you were sleeping, Maha. Everyone was talking about the date. I'm still confused. What does it mean to us?" Subba asked.

Maha dozed off to sleep, and so did Subba.

A big sound of crackers erupted as the train entered Dasiguda station, the last station in Orissa. Maha and Subba looked around. There were lights and crackers everywhere, with people playing dholks and dancing. Everyone started hugging each other. A middle-aged man started distributing sweets to everyone on the train.

"Mubarak ho, Mubarak," he shouted with joy.

"At last, after 150 years, our country is ours. Jai Hind!"

"Mubarak, Mubarak"... everyone started singing Jana Gana Mana, and all others joined in. The train slowly started towards Visakhapatnam.

"Inshallah... Bharat is free now!" Subba shouted.

Maha closed her mouth and said, "Dear Saba Ali, be like Subba Lakshmi until we reach a place where there are no signs of carnage. India has gained freedom, but not for us women." She winked at me.

She was so right!

As the train moved forward with the chants of patriotic songs, both Subba Lakshmi (Saba Ali) and Maha Lakshmi were waiting to see what lay ahead.

*As India stepped into the dawn of freedom, it was already welcomed by the bloodshed of Hindu-Muslim communal riots, starting in Bengal.

SAMAY SAMAY

"Sir, please step into the hall; you are not allowed to stand in the lobby," a strong voice snapped me back to reality. I took a few hesitant steps into the large hall, guided by the firm hands of the guards in black suits who gently nudged me forward.

I shrugged his hand off and turned back. The two guards were gigantic, like Thor meeting roided WWE champions—definitely not someone to mess with.

Where am I??? The last thing I remember was heading to an interview somewhere... *How did I get here...?*

Was it because of Uber... or was I drunk in broad daylight?

"Where *am* I???" I muttered, searching my pockets for my phone. I found my iPhone, but the screen was shattered and the time frozen at 4:31 PM.

"Gosh! One lakh rupees... What do I tell Richa now? She'll kill me over this alone."

Where am I??? A sudden idea struck me—I could ask people around me about this place. A smile crept across my face, but it vanished as quickly as it came.

Why do I remember Richa and the fear I have of her, but not something basic, like asking people questions?

Something's wrong.

I tried taking a deep breath, something I do before getting into action, but my lungs felt shallow and inadequate. I struggled to inhale—there was barely any air around.

What the...?!

With great difficulty, I managed to breathe in a little air, feeling life slowly returning to my body. My mind began to work again, and I started observing my surroundings.

"What is this place??"

It seemed like a large recruitment fair, but for only, one company. The hall was arranged in a classroom-style seating, where most people sat, staring into space. A woman in a business suit sobbed with her eyes wide open, but then she abruptly stopped crying and started looking into thin air.

I counted—34 people. A few Americans, possibly a Japanese, some blacks - Africans? This is such a global hunt huh!!

My God, is this recruitment for a global firm? Or are they recruiting for some... intelligence service? Or is this a PAN world movie by SSR?

Questions flooded my mind, but I felt relieved—at least my brain was working.

I walked toward the centre table, where a group of executives sat, busy with their laptops, their faces reading *Do Not Disturb.* But one gentleman, mild-mannered and decent-looking, seemed approachable—perhaps a customer service representative. I approached him.

He wore a black, triple-breasted suit, his eyes fixed on a paper in front of him. I tried to glance at it, but the paper was blank.

Puzzled, I asked, "Excuse me, sir, what is this—" Before I could finish my sentence, he cut me off.

"Mr. Samay, you're in the right place. Just give us some time to assess if you're the right candidate. Until then, feel free to enjoy the grand buffet we've arranged for you in the corner," he said, without even looking up.

How does he know my name?! I asked myself, aloud.

I stood there, waiting to see if he would speak again, but without raising his head, he pointed toward the corner. I turned around quickly and started walking.

Now the Sherlock Holmes in me awoke, trying to look for clues or signs. Behind the centre table, I saw two large sign boards with arrows pointing in different directions: *This Way* and *That Way.*

On my way to the buffet, I tried talking to a couple of the Americans, but it was no use. They remained in their blank, trance-like state. I hurried over to the buffet table.

It was an impressive spread: South Indian, Chinese, Mexican, Lebanese, North Indian. Mouthwatering, ideally, but I had a serious case of the cotton mouth. *Am I even hungry?* I asked my stomach. No response.

I grabbed a large steak and, with no table manners, started munching on it. After some effort, I managed to swallow a bit. That's when I noticed a tall sardarji staring at me in amazement.

He had a chicken kabab in his hand, attempting to eat it just as awkwardly as I had. He walked over to me with a smile.

"Sirji, in my town, I'm the eating champion—chutki mein ek-do murghiya uda jata hoon. But aaj pata nahi, what's happening to me. Kha hi nahi paa raha. You at least managed to eat a bit. Badiya hai ji," he said.

I was frozen in surprise—finally, someone speaking to me after what felt like ages.

He put the half-eaten kabab back on his plate and shook my hand.

"Myself Gurvinder, from Chandigarh. I don't know how I ended up here," he said, scratching his turban.

"Mr. Gurvinder, same here. I don't understand—how did we get here? Were we abducted? If so, by whom? This place doesn't seem like that. At first, I thought it was a recruitment fair, but the people at the central table aren't talking. They seem busy, as if they're writing about our lives. What do 'This Way' and 'That Way' mean? Are they washrooms? And most importantly, can I even piss? Is anything functioning properly? It felt like a war to breathe! Are we being drafted into some sort of army? What's happening??"

Gurvinder looked at me, as puzzled as I was.

"Sirji, ye sab jo bhi hai, I just hope they send us back soon. Wohi mere liye badhiya hoga ji! My daughter's wedding is… soon — today, tomorrow, or sometime very soon."

Gurvinder's words began to trail off. He didn't seem as energetic as before. We walked around, searching for anyone else acting strangely like us.

I spotted a woman in her 30s throwing a tantrum. She looked like a model… or had I seen her in a film? I tried to recall her name. *Superstar Sanjana Kapoor…* yes! What was she doing here?

I also noticed an elderly man, around 70, arguing loudly.

"Do you know who I am? I'm the minister of…," he hesitated, "I can't remember the name of my state, but I'm a big man. I have contacts everywhere! I'll see the end of you!"

Ugh, so much drama. I walked towards a wall and stood by it. Gurvinder sat on a nearby chair, watching me.

"Alert, everyone!" A voice, strong like an earthquake, shook the room. Heads, starting with mine, turned toward the sound.

We all stood.

"Please come to the center of the room, stand straight, and wait for my next instruction," the voice commanded.

"I've never stood in line, even in school," Sanjana muttered from behind me.

I smiled at her comment and obediently stood in the first row, in the first position. I'd always wanted to be first, in school, in life—even though I had no idea what I was standing for now.

A small unrest began in the crowd, but then a 6.5-foot man in a black suit strode in with thumping footsteps.

"Silence!"

"Well, to this office, entry is granted by invitation and destiny. Soon, you'll cross this clearance line to either Zone A or Zone B. But first, I have to ask you a few questions. Your responses will determine your next step forward."

A quiz, huh? I told myself. My heart raced, and I could feel the blood rushing through my body.

"My first question: Which country are you from?"

"I'm from India!" I shouted, raising my hand.

"Born in India, but I'm officially a Canadian citizen," Sanjana added.

"Sirji, Sector-36, Chandigarh, Punjab, India. Pin code, bhool gaya ji," Gurvinder said.

I heard "New York, America" from one corner.

"My second question: Which year were you born?"

"1983. Do you want me to tell you the date and time too?" I asked, stepping forward and raising my hand.

"19…," Sanjana stammered, unsure of her answer.

"My last question: Do you remember the last face you saw before you found yourself here?"

Silence filled the room. Even Gurvinder and Sanjana had gone pale.

I closed my eyes, trying to remember. I took a deep breath and, with tears in my eyes, spoke.

"My mother and my wife… they gave me a tearful send-off. The last thing I remember was watching a video of my little one's first steps toward me, with my mom and wife cheering him on. He fell twice, cried, then stood up with the help of a wall. He walked toward me, and just before he reached my feet, he fell again, giggling."

I cried aloud, and the room fell silent again.

"All of you, walk toward me. Except you, Samay. Please step toward the entrance. My team will escort you," the man ordered.

I couldn't believe what was happening. The others began walking in straight lines toward him, like machines. Gurvinder briefly turned and stared at me with no expression—completely blank.

The two strong hands that had pushed me into the hall now gently guided me out and made me stand on a green circle.

"Mister, I don't know your name, but you were—" Suddenly, they pushed me, and I stood on the green circle.

"Mister, I don't know your name.. But you were… rudeeeeeeeeeeeeeeeeeeeeeeeee", they pushed me as I stood on that green circle.

***

"A Tragic Flight accident which happened earlier in the morning, the flight with passengers of 34 which is flying from Chennai to New Delhi, has only one survivor. Mr. Samay Sharma – a Creative Director in Chennai, has luckily survived this accident with no injuries. He woke up from a temporary coma after 6 hours."

"Our crew tried to connect with Samay Sharma at the hospital. He kept narrating about a big hall where the people were inducted into worlds beyond. Either we should credit his storytelling skills of being a creative director or credit his fate of survival to an almighty force. The mystery remains in the fact that Samay has still samay in him.

We will get back to you with more groundbreaking reports. Keep watching us TV Today."

WISH I COULD…….

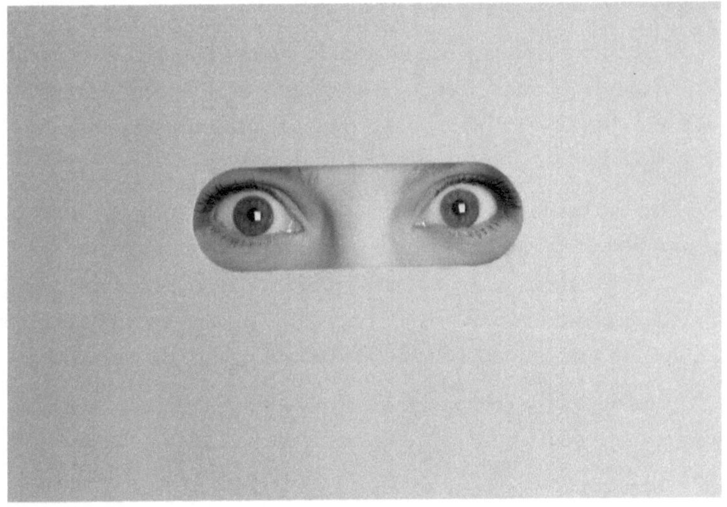

Ajeeb daastaan hai yeh

Kahan shuru kahan khatam

Yeh manzile hai kaunsi

Na voh samajh sake na…

The major's voice hit my ears, painfully out of tune. Such a bad singer. I wish I could tell him, but I'm too scared of how he might react. I wish we could speak the same language—then I could say, "Dude, you have the gift of scaring the hell out of everyone with just your voice. You know that, right? Wish you were on mute."

"Tarun!" he shouted. I ran towards him. "Out!" I quickly followed his orders and stepped out of the room. A few minutes later, a woman with a strong fragrance walked in. The major hugged and kissed her, shutting the door in my face.

I turned towards the courtyard, trying to distract myself from whatever was happening inside.

If the major was hungry, couldn't he just grab something from the fridge? Why does he always eat off her mouth?

My attention drifted to the apartment across from ours. Odd smell. Mr. Iyer was sneaking something behind his coat as he went inside. His wife was away visiting her mother, so he was probably preparing for a "bachelor's bash."

The flat below Mr. Iyer's belonged to Pammy Aunty, the loudest gossip monger in the community—and she hates me. Every time she sees me, her expression shifts from a grin to irritation in a heartbeat. No one suspects her, but I know she's been stealing valuables left carelessly around. She's sneaky enough to avoid getting caught by the cameras, too.

Then there's the group of voyeurs, always lurking, always leering at women—age no bar.

God, I hate their stares.

And then there's Ms. Grewal, the community's eye candy. Even I'm a fan. Wow, she smells incredible! Everyone's heart skips a beat when she steps out of her door and walks toward her car. No one really knows what she does for a living.

The corrupted community president, Mr. Shanmugam; the sleepwalker, Ali; Mr. Alpha Male, Jatin; Zombie Lal, our security officer—what a fake bunch. They say something, but they show something completely different on the outside. Do they ever confess? God knows.

Suddenly, I heard shouting from the first floor and saw Mr. Lal coming down the stairs.

He was screaming at his wife, "How long has this been going on? I got a tip that someone's been visiting you when I'm not around."

His voice was loud, but his heart was pounding. She stayed calm, even though it was obvious she was caught. I'd always suspected something was up.

"Do you want to know who it was?" she retorted loudly, making him fall silent.

"I wanted to tell you earlier, but I didn't want to ruin his life. I warned him three times, but he didn't listen."

"It was Anuj. He's been sneaking into our house while you're away, and he tried to force himself on me."

She pointed at a frail, innocent-looking young man standing in the crowd—Anuj. He looked shell-shocked.

"I would never do such a thing," he stammered, struggling to defend himself.

Mr. Lal's wife slapped him hard, cutting him off. Then the unthinkable happened.

The crowd pounced on Anuj, kicking and punching him, including Mr. Lal. Anuj lay bloodied on the ground, semi-conscious, his eyes locking with mine.

We looked at each other for a long moment.

All the questions have answers—even this one. But will Anuj dare to speak up?

Is Mrs. Lal seeing someone else? Yes.

Did Anuj try to meet Mrs. Lal? Yes.

Did he try to molest her? No.

It was all a ploy by Mrs. Lal to deflect attention and make Anuj the scapegoat.

How do I know?

Anuj had confided in me weeks ago, when we were in the park. He sat next to me and started talking.

At first, I thought it was just the usual blabber, like how major keeps telling me stuff all the time. But then Anuj made a dark confession.

"I wish I could tell this to the world, but neither of us— me or the world— are strong enough to bear the truth. You're the first to know this, and I have shared this with you as I know you won't let this out to the world" he said.

"I'm a woman trapped in a man's body. I keep asking myself 'why' and 'how,' but all I know is that I want to be a woman, not a man. Do you understand?"

I nodded.

"Throw this bastard out of the community," Mr. Lal ordered the security guard.

I wish I could yell out the truth, but in this world full of dark lies, the simple truth doesn't stand a chance.

"Tarun!" the major's voice called again. I turned towards our house. The major stepped out, followed by the woman. She had left abruptly.

I walked towards the major. The woman's beautiful fragrance was gone—now she smelled sweaty and exhausted. They must have fought.

"Tarun, here. Eat." The major pushed my food plate toward me.

I ran to it and started eating wiggling my tail.

"Good dog," he said, rubbing my head.

Oh, by the way, Taruni is his ex-wife's name. He named me 'Tarun' after her.

He resumed singing in that painfully irritating tone,

Ajeeb daastaan hai yeh...

But I wasn't listening to his terrible singing anymore. My eyes were on the food, but my mind was full of questions and answers—I wish I could say them aloud!

AT THE TURN OF...........

How can a man escape his predetermined fate? How can he defy destiny?

I am a subject of destiny. I believe everyone is—sons and daughters of the Creator, though the name of our creators may vary from person to person. I have my own creator, and he has defined who I am and how my life will unfold. Every twist and turn etched into the fabric of time.

Born into a wealthy family in the fractured USSR, I am a reigning prince of a royal clan that crumbled. The communists, backed by the government, conspired to overthrow our mighty power, we held on the block.

That night was a nightmare, a bloodbath that tore my family apart.

Thirty-four members of my family, including my father, were brutally murdered. Their bodies were riddled with bullets, victims of a senseless massacre. That night is a violent dance of death orchestrated by Vepr-12s, Saiga-12s and SV-98s. A downpour of bullets that pierced every inch of the family member in a whiff.

I tried to escape with my siblings, but my brother was wounded, a 12-gauge bullet tearing apart his right calf. We hid in a marshy pond, clinging to life until the raiders finally left.

Emerging from the water, drenched and gasping for air, I looked at my siblings—my sister in shock, my brother weeping silently. I was too numb to feel pain, my body a vessel of suffering.

Shards of glass had pierced my flesh, leaving me in agony. My body cried out for rest, but my mind was consumed by a burning desire for revenge.

"Boris! You have to live this night somehow!"

"What is he going to do?" a strange voice echoed in Suresh's head.

Was it real, or was it a figment of my imagination? His mind started wavering beyond balance.

After moments of confusion, Suresh realized his fate was dependent on him

What has Suresh got to do with this?

Who is he??

Suresh Murugan, a 31 years old, from Tiruchirapalli, Tamil Nadu, India. He is still unmarried. By nature, Suresh is an introvert and has had very few friends since his childhood. He was often bullied in school and always felt like an outsider. In his free time, evenings, and holidays, he spent quality time with his family, a typical working-class Indian family whose greatest ambition is to own a home and save 10 lakhs rupees by the age of 58. Suresh grew up with this mindset and believed that contentment is the greatest gift life has to offer.

Until he met his first love, Chandra Kala, his neighbor's daughter. When he mustered the courage to express his feelings for her, she rejected him outright, labeling him a loser, lacking confidence, and unable to speak English. This profound rejection left a deep wound on Suresh's heart and spirit. He retreated to his room for days, while everyone feared he was becoming depressed or contemplating something drastic.

But Suresh wasn't thinking about the end. He was searching for inspiration, something to ignite a spark within him, a kick on his butt! And that's when he found his first true friend—a book. And that's when he met me.

"What is he going to do?" Suresh said to himself again. "This seems like the end of the road for Boris. Just like me, what is he going to do?" he shouted so loudly that it almost shattered my eardrums, his voice echoing through the room

I was uncertain about my future. At this crucial point in my life, what would happen to me? Would I be killed by those hunting warlords before dawn, or would I hunt them down like a wounded lion seeking my revenge?

Just then, Suresh pressed pause on my unending thoughts, marking the page.

He got up to answer the door.

"Suresha! What's going on? Won't you come out?" his mother's worried voice echoed through the room.

"No, Amma! I need to finish this book—it's really interesting. It's called 'The Boris Path.' It's about a wounded son of a royal clan tycoon seeking revenge for his family's death. Every line fills me with confidence and a strength I didn't know I had."

Meanwhile, I was still crouched behind the stones, taking care of my siblings, waiting for Suresh to return!

At the turn of the next page, something powerful, something unseen ever before moment happened, as I, the Boris looked between the rock cracks into the eyes of Suresh.

At the turn of…

THIN LINE BETWEEN L & D

Before you take your final breath, there are a few crucial moments in your life that will flash before your eyes like a quick montage. This happens to everyone, both humans and animals. My mother always spoke about this moment to our 50 brothers.

In our community, many people have faced near-death experiences and miraculously survived at the last moment. My mother was one of them. She always told me to conserve my energy for the most crucial moments—those near-death situations. Unfortunately, we have these moments every half hour. In fact, I have lost all my brothers in a blink of an eye.

All 50 of them, except me!

It might sound unreal to you, but it's true!

Born near the gritty slums of Mumbai, I never travelled towards the uptown among the affluent society. My Mom always warned me, "Beta, beware of those places, we are the last ones on this planet they want to see and they do everything it takes to nail us down and throw like we are nothing. My mom spoke from experience, having witnessed the harsh deaths of my siblings.

"But, Mom, the food there is delicious, I heard?"

"Forget about the food, do you want to stay alive in the first place or not?" my mom shouted back.

"Of course, I want to, but even here, we barely survive day by day. Remember Mota Khan, he used to bully me every day. He disappeared, and so did his dad. That happened just down our street." I paused to see my mom's reaction.

"So, what I'm trying to say is, Mom, whether we're here or there, we're all going to die eventually. But let me try that delicious food before I go." I turned back and stepped out, moving quickly before my mom could call me back.

My gang of friends sneaked into that neighborhood, the one everyone in my community talked about. It had luxurious houses, green lawns, and amazing food. As we slipped over the wall into a large villa, I saw something I had never seen before in my small life. Healthy people were walking around on the lawn, laughing, and dancing to music.

"Yummy, food it is!" my frail friend exclaimed, licking his lips as I looked at him.

Sure, a feast for him and me too. It's been two days since we've had proper food. The ghost smoke in our neighborhood scared the hell out of us.

"Now it was the time to binge on food and stay alive for a few more days", I thought to myself. We slowly sneaked onto the lawn, searching for a quiet spot.

There was a girl sitting on a chair, staring into thin air and puffing smoke into the air.

"Look at her! A great meal," I thought to myself as I approached her.

I stood behind her, my hands slowly reaching for her neck.

Then the unexpected happened. Something in the air, like a chemical, caused me to faint.

My mom's words of caution echoed in my ears.

I crashed onto the floor, my vision fading as I looked up.

The same happened to my friend. He was already down, but not moving at all.

"Farewell, dost!"

I waited for a few more moments and then tried to escape from the place as quickly as possible.

Two hands grabbed me from both sides, and I fell down.

Laughter erupted around me. "Ek machar sala admi ko………!" "What a dialogue, Nanaji. You're great!"

"Dude, whenever I kill a mosquito, I remind myself of this line."

GULAAB JAMUN FRIENDS

"Janaab, Mr. Sharma has arrived," the Head of Security informed Mr. Ameer, who was engrossed in important documents.

Mr. Ameer looked up with a serious expression. "How could he just show up like that, without an appointment?" he raised his voice, startling the Head of Security.

"Sir, but Mr. Sharma wasn't listening..."

"Arey Ameer Bhai, if I need to meet you, do I need to follow a protocol? Did you follow the protocol when you sneaked into my house for your favorite Gulab Jamun? You never left a single piece for me, even in my own house," Mr. Sharma said, entering the room and sitting on the sofa in front of Mr. Ameer.

He grinned mockingly at Mr. Ameer, trying to stifle his laughter. Turning to the Head of Security, he imitated his voice and said, "Your PM Saab is always short-tempered since our school days. All he needs is a couple of kicks on his butt, which I'm good at giving. Meanwhile, you go and get two strong cups of chai for both of us."

As soon as the security guard left, Mr. Ameer started laughing at Mr. Sharma. "Asshole, why did you remind me of Gulab Jamun? My mouth is watering. When you came from there, why didn't you bring me a box?"

"Sweet revenge, this is what it is!" Mr. Sharma winked at him.

"When is your team coming to our land? It's been a while since we defeated you and had a celebratory festival," Mr. Sharma taunted Mr. Ameer.

"Whoa, look who's talking. You've never handled our bowling. After you became the PM, we haven't had a festival in our streets since defeating you on your own turf," Mr. Ameer retorted instantly.

Mr. Sharma stood up and started walking.

"Tillu, you've lost it. You could never win over me in debates, let alone a match. Hahahaha!" Mr. Ameer guffawed in his chair.

Unexpectedly, Mr. Sharma threw a rubber ball at Mr. Ameer, shouting "Catch!" Mr. Ameer missed the ball, and it hit him straight on the forehead.

Mr. Sharma laughed uncontrollably for the next five minutes, leaving Mr. Ameer red-faced with anger.

"You can't even catch that ball, and you call yourself the greatest player of our times? Your team is a bunch of super heroes. Hahahaha! First, learn to catch, then think about winning matches," Mr. Sharma said in his usual loud tone, acting childishly.

"Ahaa, okay, I'll show you who's who now. You pick up that bat and take my fastest delivery." Mr. Ameer said, rubbing the ball against his groin.

Even Mr. Sharma became serious at the challenge, stood up, and took the bat from the corner.

Mr. Ameer and Mr. Sharma exchanged fierce looks for a moment. Then Mr. Ameer prepared to deliver the fastest pitch.

Mr. Sharma took his stance, ready to smash the ball. Just as Mr. Ameer was about to bowl, his mother's voice echoed from a distance.

"Ameer! Where are you, beta? It's already late for lunch. Get the sheep back home. If I miss any one of the sheep, I'll skin you alive!"

Ameer turned towards his mother and started running towards the sheep that were scattered everywhere.

"Are oh Sharma, we'll continue this tomorrow. The ball is with me. Get me the Gulab Jamun, please," Ameer shouted as he disappeared into the bushes.

Sharma looked at Ameer, across the border. With a disappointed expression, he pulled up his slipping shorts and started walking towards his home.

A typical day of two wannabe Prime Ministers, but still innocent bachas across the borders!

MY WORLD AROUND...

Today marks the end of a beautiful chapter in my life. If I were to share this with my parents or confide in my sister, they would likely scold me. The irony is, I can't. They have every right to say anything; after all, they were my caregivers until now. They were my hands and legs, guiding me through the world. For a time, I borrowed their most important sense, their vision, to understand the world.

But they say, "When God takes away something, he always leaves a gift behind." That gift allowed me to perceive people and the world in a way that most people can't. I experienced the world more intimately than anyone else.

Normal people are so judgmental, so opinionated about others and their situations. My sister's friend Jay was a regular visitor to our house. I had never spoken to him except for the first time. But I know he came for me. He made sure to sit near me and observed me without saying a word.

I could have told him to leave or yelled at him. But there was something about him. I sensed that he wasn't just looking at me; he was trying to communicate with me. Strangely, we seemed to have a conversation without speaking, without really our lips moving.

Silence used to rule whenever we met at our place. My dad considered Jay an unpleasant, uninvited guest with ulterior motives. He warned my sister not to let him visit anymore. The last time Jay came, it caused a big mess, as my dad strongly warned him to stay away.

Jay didn't utter a word. But he had a lot to say to me. I rejected his final words as he was about to leave our home. I felt sad after he left.

A few more moments of my journey in that colorful world were about to end. I might not look at people like Jay as normal people do. I might react, overreact, and judge. I might become just another fool in the maddening crowd.

"Now, slowly open your eyes, Madhu!" the doctor said, in a soothing tone. I struggled to open my eyes. After a little effort, I opened them—only to see the world in black and white. My dad, my mom, my sister, the nurse, and the doctor were all there. As I turned around to look at the room, everything was in black and white. The colors in my life had faded. I sighed to myself.

"How is the world through your eyes, Madhu?" a familiar voice asked from my right. I knew it was Jay. My eyes welled up with tears, but I didn't look at him. He came towards me and sat on the bed, dressed in a linen blue shirt and dark blue chinos. He kissed my forehead and said, "Now I will live through your beautiful soul."

"I always misunderstood Jay," my dad said to my mom, his eyes filled with tears. "How rude I was to throw him out of the house that day?"

"Jay must be happy wherever he is, as his last wish is fulfilled," my sister added.

I overheard their conversation while looking at Jay. He stepped out of the room and stopped, turning to look at me with a smile. "Let's see."

My eyes still saw the world in black and white, but that didn't matter to my heart.

YOUR DREAMS ARE MINE....

I stepped outside the main door, looking around with a sense of bewilderment. The day was sunny, but the heat and intensity didn't seem to affect the faces around me. As I observed the crowd, I saw a mix of emotions: relaxation, happiness, relief, some smiles, and some tears—all of which make us human.

What about me? How was I feeling? Was it the shock mixed with unending disappointment, a lingering sense of surprise, or perhaps anger directed at myself? As I slowly walked towards my car, my mind raced with countless thoughts.

Who was I? Where was I now? Keeki was a successful marketing professional who had made a name for herself in less than a year. She was the most sought-after person in the company, celebrated and admired. Don't mess with Keeki. She was more powerful and dangerous than her boss. If she had a grudge, she could ruin your career.

In short, Keeki was ambitious, ruthless, charming yet dangerous, domineering, and a highly performing marketing professional.

"Are you really that Keeki?" I asked myself in the mirror as I drove.

"A mean bitch?"

Tears rolled down my cheeks. I turned the car to the side to check my mascara and prevent it from smudging. Wiping away my tears carefully, I told myself, "Girl, get a hold of yourself. Your lunch meeting with Hendricks is crucial. It's not just another meeting; it's your opportunity to secure the next big position. Don't forget about the memorable evening ahead. You can do this. These feelings are nonsense. Remember what you're here for."

My attention turned to the package Dev had given me.

"Dev!"

My eyes became clouded with tears again, his name on my tongue and his charming face in my mind.

The world knew me as the 'Mean Bitch', but who was I really? And Dev knew it perfectly. In fact, he had discovered the beautiful side of me when I was just a small-town innocent named Keerthana Kishan.

I was the quietest girl, always sitting in the front row for two years of our engineering college, when Dev first met me. He was the most dynamic and popular student in the college, a well-balanced genius and prankster. Dev encountered me for the first time during the ragging or junior introduction. I was standing nervously on the platform surrounded by our seniors.

They asked me to sing and dance, but I froze with fear. If the seniors had made any more requests or demands, I would have fainted right there.

"Tell us this, and you can go," a strong voice came from behind. I looked at him. It was Dev.

"If God asked you to focus all your energy, passion, and attention on one thing, what would it be?"

Hundreds of heads turned towards Dev and then back to me with surprise. I looked at everyone with newfound confidence from within. "My first book," I replied.

"My thoughts and hidden words can overcome this fear and create a beautiful portrayal of a beautiful character," I said.

The seniors burst into laughter, but Dev continued to look at me as I left the room.

A few days later, while I was in the library, I heard a voice behind me. "Ms. Rowling," Dev said, leaning over me. I became alert at his presence.

"Ms. Rowling is like you, except she turned her childhood fantasies into Harry Potter. I'm curious to know what your story will be. You're like a superhero, saving the world," he winked at me.

I blushed instantly but managed to control myself.

"It's all about Keerthana, but with a different, sweet, and cute name. It's about her journey of the heart, her unexplored experiences, and her love life. Why should I tell you? You can buy the book when it's released," I replied.

As I tried to leave, Dev held my hand and said, "I love you."

"These three words are precious to me, so I've never used them before. I feel you're the best person to hear them," he said.

Before Dev could say anything else, I left the hall without looking back.

For the next few days, I tried to avoid Dev, which I'm sure irritated him.

"What's wrong with you, Keeki?" Dev's voice sounded weak. I turned to look at him. At first glance, I was worried by his frail appearance but didn't let the feeling surface.

"Don't ever call me Keeki. It's a stupid name, Dev. I have a name that I like. And don't try so hard to impress me. Trust me, it won't work."

"Look, Dev, we come from different worlds. While joy and fun rule your side, fear and insecurity dominate mine. I came here to study responsibly, not for fun or to search for love. You might say that if I don't experience love, how can I write a book about it? Dev, that was my deepest desire. I hope to fulfill it when my inner quest finds the real thing."

"For God's sake, please don't bring this topic up again. If you want to be a good friend, please," I said.

I still remember Dev's reaction. I don't know how to describe it, but it was the face of a defeated man who might give up on life.

But I didn't look back to apologize.

Years after graduating and enrolling in a management course, I was invited to an alumni meet, which I kept skipping, knowing I would have to face Dev. I received messages from friends about Dev asking for my whereabouts and contact number.

Did I hate Dev? No, I didn't.

Years later, I was happy to hear about Dev's success in the U.S. owning his own firm. But I felt sad that he never got married.

Feelings for him resurfaced during that time but were quickly dismissed when I entered the corporate world as a trainee in a small-time PR agency in Mumbai. I felt suffocated and breathless. I assumed every man around me was lusting after me and trying to touch or tease me in the name of corporate culture.

I cried many times in my hostel all night long. I couldn't go back. I couldn't face my father. I ran away from the town to chase my dreams, leaving them behind. In fact, I had nowhere to go except... dying.

Every morning until evening, I had to hide from the ultimate predator in the office, my boss. He was ruthless yet had a soft spot for me (soft meant overly caring, trying to seduce). He ensured from behind the curtains that I faced struggles so that I would have to go to him.

I wanted to scream from the bottom of my heart and kick him, but I never had the courage. If I had had the courage, I would have faced my dad and convinced him. If I had had the courage, I would have accepted Dev. I was a coward.

But things started to change within me, slowly. Survival of the fittest, as the law of nature dictates, I had to fight with myself before confronting these bastards. The fight began with changing myself, killing the real me: innocent, kind, and beautiful. I built an alter ego and that ego consumed me. I named it Keeki. I named myself Keeki.

I will never forget the day of my unleashing. My boss, already offended and figuring I was a tough nut to crack, started scolding and humiliating me in front of clients and even the junior staff.

I held back my anger and rage for that day. And then that day came!

I was presenting the client revenue map to everyone, sharing my ideas and activities to increase revenue from my accounts. Everything went well. Seeing the positive nods on everyone's faces, I felt happy inside and returned to my seat.

My boss was silent and furious.

"Look, Keerthana! If you think that by showing slides and some graphs to me, I will be convinced, then you're wrong. The numbers you promised are still far off. As an account director, you always have to outperform yourself. If you repeat this bloody fucking performance, I will fuck you right here on this table and destroy your confidence," he said.

That made me mad, super mad. Suddenly, I stood on the chair, threw everything on the table, and sat on it with my legs wide open.

"Come on! F*** me, try touching me, you p***. I dare you. F*** you, menopausal bastard," I shouted.

He was in deep shock, his face devoid of blood. He was panicked, perhaps paralyzed, as were everyone else in the room. What had happened to Keerthana?

"BTW, I'm not Keerthana, I'm Keeki," I said before storming out of the room and out of the office.

There was no looking back. After resigning from the company, I received numerous offers, mostly from my boss's haters.

From then on, I kept my heart in a locker, no room for emotions or sentiments. My presence in the office was a threat to my subordinates, a blockade to my bosses, but a boon to the revenues.

"Unstoppable Keeki," people used to say. In fact, I became so popular in Mumbai's PR circuit.

Life these days was all by my choice, and I was the master.

So many men, starting with bosses, tried to impress me. But I kept them away, knowing where they wanted to end up. Amidst all this, I never forgot two things: my dream book—a portrayal of myself as a beautiful angel—and Dev.

The angel within me was already dead, and the red-hot bitch was ruling. In moments of solitude and peace, I always tried to start the first page of my book but never got past two lines. Yet, my visualizations of Keerthana remained somewhere within me, creating every line of the story, but Keeki wasn't letting it out.

And Dev. I wished I could see him once. Hear him once. Know what was in his heart.

On October 14th, my birthday, I was planning a party for my team at Hyatt. I received a call from Dev, saying he wanted to meet me. I was overjoyed inside but didn't let it show. I told him to meet at Starbucks in Bandra West.

The initial moments were awkward as we sat silently. But I couldn't help but look at him. He looked so mature and balanced.

"Look at you. Where was that innocent Keerthana?" he winked at me.

"Keeki," I replied.

"My name is Keeki now," I said with a smile. A genuine smile for him, the first one in many years.

I could see him blushing instantly.

"Keeki, I don't want to repeat the nonsense you don't want to hear. I have a humble request. I came here all the way to see you. Spend some time with me. I have three more days to be around. If not as my girlfriend, then as an old friend, will you spend some time with me during these three days, please?"

I didn't want to refuse. After all, he was the reason for whatever girl happiness I had in my life so far. I owed him.

The next three days were like a dream, a fast-paced dream. We spent time happily. Every moment of those 72 hours was filled with energy, happiness, and unshared love for each other. Dev didn't touch me even once, while I was yearning for his first touch and kiss. He brought Keerthana back to life.

Dev left after that, leaving behind bundles of sweet memories. During one of the days, while we were at Kushal's grape estate, he asked, "Is your dream book still on, Keeki?"

"It's in here, Dev," I pointed to my head. "It will always be a dream project, in my dreams." I laughed.

Dev kept looking at me and said, "No, Keeki, it has already started. I guess you have to figure out how to end it. Trust me."

I brushed off his words.

"Accomplished PR Head of the Year by NNC Group" was an award the entire media world waited for. And this year, I was about to receive it. The entire company was proud of me, and since morning, my phone had been flooded with calls and messages. My afternoon meeting with my super boss would also decide my future at the company. Would I be the next big boss for the country operations? Two milestones that would shape my life forever.

But one call that morning made me go to Nanavati Hospital to see Dev.

"Adenocarcinoma stomach cancer, Stage IV," the doctor said.

"I met him a month ago, doctor. He was perfectly fine," I replied in disbelief.

"You know about cancer. You never know until it's there. He knew he had cancer six months ago. Maybe he's ready for it. Until yesterday morning, he could talk," the doctor said.

"He gave this mobile to you. He has a message for you in it, and this package he wanted you to have," the doctor said before leaving the room.

"Can I see him, doctor?" I asked with a broken voice and tears in my eyes.

"Actually, he didn't want that. Sorry about that," he sighed and left.

I understood Dev. I left the hospital for my flat to see what was in the video and the package.

I closed all the doors and sat on the floor once I reached home. I switched off my mobile and kept it away.

My hands reached for his mobile to play the video. There was only one video in the gallery, and it was for me.

"Dear Keeki, the feeling of fresh love didn't leave me even until today, and your memories of our first meeting are still lingering in my mind. Though we are not destined for each other, my heart was destined to have your love. Nevertheless, during all those days without you, I have built a beautiful dream of yours, where I have followed you wherever you went and surprisingly, I have found you and your story," the video began.

"The book is a parting gift for you, to unite yourself with yourself. As I said, how to end this story is truly in your hands. Love you forever," the video ended.

I cried uncontrollably, wishing for his hand to hold me closer and console me.

I slowly opened the package and took out the book.

The first page started with a line: "YOUR DREAMS ARE MY DREAMS."

My heart had always said this to me. I was a loner, but he proved it wrong.

I was shocked. That was a line I had written years ago. As I read through page after page, I realized Dev had written every line of my heart, every line I yearned to write. He depicted every visual as if he had followed me on every path and turn.

I couldn't believe my eyes. Was it possible?

My heart said it was.

As I reached the last page, I noticed two lines in red ink:

"Keeki, take over. Don't let your story be decided by fate. Write your own.

"WHO ARE YOU, DEV?????????, I love you!!!!!!! Please don't leave me... please..." This is gut wrenching. Oh god, please undo this. Please!!!!!

THE SON OF A MAN

"Saala Kismat" – a common phrase I hear from my Indian friend. It often irritates me with its helpless tone and endless complaints, but now it seems fitting for my current situation.

I've always lived life as a hero, feeling on top of the world with admirers, followers, and haters alike. My family and neighbors believe I'm special, a belief that's been ingrained since birth.

Our community is renowned for its architects and builders. While I don't know the extent of our influence, my dad insists everyone admires our architectural prowess. Yet, my friends claim we're treated with disdain by the neighborhood and especially the uptown crowd. Some even have an allergic reaction to our presence. It bothers me, but I drown my sorrows in alcohol. Life isn't about complaining and dwelling on the past.

My reputation precedes my incredible building skills. I've gained fame and admiration, particularly among women. Every Friday night is a new adventure, often leading to street brawls over girls. While I enjoy my rebellious nature, my parents believe I'm becoming a spoiled brat.

"Son, when the best in our community can build a building complex in less than four hours, you're the only one who can build five in less than an hour," my dad once said. "This is a remarkable gift. I want you to meet your uncle, Manhattan South, on Friday. He'll guide you. Remember, he has a short temper."

"But Dad, Friday? I have a party downtown," I thought to myself. I wanted to object, but this was the first time he'd asked me to do something. I decided to make him happy for Friday.

The two days before Friday were unusual. I wasn't my usual self. I couldn't explain why. I had sleepless nights, and my friends teased me, "You must be dreaming about that girl downtown. So many dreams, so much hard work." I remained silent, confused by my own turmoil. I had a bad feeling about the Friday meeting.

"Eddie, want to join me to meet my uncle?" I asked.

"Manhattan South sounds adventurous. I'm in. While you're busy with your uncle, I'll prank those fools. Manhattan guys hate us, don't they?"

For a moment, I forgot my worries and laughed.

Three hours later, as we entered the premises from behind, we couldn't find my uncle. We waited in a corner, as my dad had instructed. "Uncle's favorite corner, I guess," I told Eddie.

"A favorite corner, huh? Ask him to get some joints, and we'll make this corner puff," Eddie whispered. We both laughed silently.

The hall was noisy, with people chatting in groups. A young man in his early twenties walked towards our corner, looking nervous. He seemed like a perfect target for Eddie's mischievous nature.

"There's our man. Until your uncle arrives, let's play with him. You're the man, why don't you do the honors?" Eddie pushed me towards him.

The mischievous side of me took over, but my eyes were still searching for my uncle. It seemed like he would take a while, so I decided to have some fun. I approached the young man from behind, and Eddie's eyes widened with excitement. I slowly placed my hands on his neck and bit him.

The young man screamed, spotted me, and ran away. Eddie laughed uncontrollably, but his laughter faded as I began to feel dizzy and weak. I fell to the floor, unconscious.

For the next few hours, I felt like I was in a dream.

"Son, what happened at the meeting? Please tell us the truth," my dad asked softly. I opened my eyes to see my mom, brother, Eddie, and the family doctor looking at me anxiously.

I looked at Eddie, but he hadn't said anything yet. I had to tell them the whole story. No one wanted to speak. Even the doctor looked at me, tried to say something, but shook his head and left my room. I was clueless.

Two days later, when I felt better, I went outside and realized the shock of my life. My gift was gone! The once-gifted architect who could build things in an instant couldn't even climb a wall.

"What the hell happened?" I wondered. "Did one bite do this to me? Did one little prank cost me my lifelong gift?"

I walked onto the street, stood against a wall, and looked at the sky. I used to bet my friends that I would build castles that touched the sky.

"Now what?"

Suddenly, wind pushed me hard. I fell to the floor and stood up quickly to check what had happened.

A young man was jumping from wall to wall, from building to building like lightning. After a few moments, he stood on top of a building and shouted with joy.

I tried hard to see his face and connect it to my forgotten past. Was he the man?

"Yes, he is!"

In a split second, the young man jumped to the ground, a few feet away from me, and started walking normally. He stopped near me, looked into a mirror where I was standing, fixed his hair, and smiled.

"Hi, I'm Peter Parker," he said to himself.

Just an inch away from the mirror, I stood in shock. "Mr. Parker – Son of a... Man. With your gifts, you became..."

Mr. Parker vanished, and I stood there, clueless and powerless.

Saala Kismat!

I AM ALWAYS THERE WITH YOU...

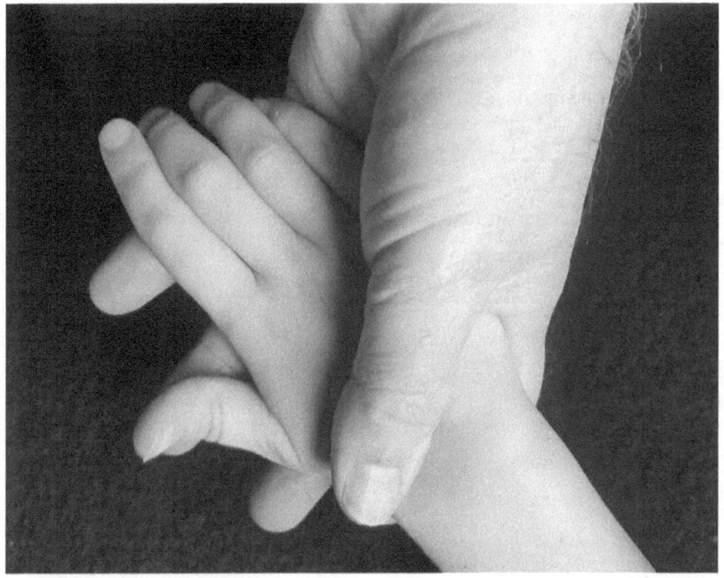

"Sorry to bother you at this time, but Abhi wanted to meet you," Prashanth said softly. In his 50s with salt-and-pepper hair, Prashanth looked younger than his age. Behind him, Abhishant and his mother, Priyanka, entered the room. A few moments later, Dr. Amish joined them, busy on a phone call.

Madhu was puzzled by the unexpected visitors. The last time she had so many guests was four months ago, a date she couldn't forget. She quickly regained her composure, cleared her throat, and greeted them, offering them seats on the sofa.

Dr. Amish looked around for a place to sit, as the only sofa was occupied. Madhu immediately offered him a stool, and he thanked her and sat down.

As Madhu was about to go to the kitchen to get water and snacks, Priyanka gently stopped her, holding her hand. With Priyanka's touch, Madhu felt calmer and looked at everyone in detail, hiding her enthusiasm.

"Who are they?" "Why are they here?" "Did Krishna owe them anything?" "Oh God! You have no mercy on me. This is not fair. How can I handle this?" Thousands of thoughts raced through her mind, and Madhu felt her hands go numb.

"Look sir, if you think I can repay what Krishna owed you, you're wrong," Madhu replied sternly. "I'm barely making ends meet. And the pain of losing him is unbearable. I have no one to take care of me. Please understand," tears streaming down her face.

While Priyanka tried to comfort her, 14-year-old Abhishant's lips trembled, and tears welled up in his eyes as he watched Madhu. He tried to speak, but no words came out.

"Madhu, we're not here to take anything from you," Prashanth said. "We know the pain and trouble you've been through. The loss of Krishna can't be replaced."

"You don't know anything, sir," Madhu replied sternly. "Krishna and I had a love marriage against our parents' wishes. We come from a village where our communities don't stand each other. The day of our marriage was also the day our families disowned us.

With great dreams and expectations, we moved to this city. I don't have much education, but Krishna had graduated. He started working in a company and earned a decent salary, giving us a good start in life. When I thought we were finally settled, Krishna made a mistake by taking out high-interest loans to buy a house. He couldn't manage the debt, and to pay off one loan, he had to take out another.

He initially hid this from me, but later he was too scared to tell me. I thought everything was fine and was waiting for him at home when an ambulance arrived with his dead body."

Madhu collapsed on the floor weeping.

"Did you or your family go through this kind of fateful torture?", Madhu uttered with pain.

"I don't know how to put this, but, Krishna's life on this earth was and will be meaningful."

"Madhu, we're here to thank you personally for what Krishna did for our family. Abhi has been suffering from a rare heart disease that required a ventilator. Doctors gave him only six days to live, and a heart transplant was the only option. We left the advanced technology in the US to bring Abhi back to his hometown for his final moments. When Krishna's accident happened and he was brought to the hospital, the man who brought him claimed to be his cousin and offered a heart transplant for a lump sum payment. The situation was so critical that we agreed, not knowing whose heart it was. Abhi was saved, and we returned to the US. When Abhi recovered, he kept asking to meet you. We were busy with our careers and postponed our visit, but Abhi became insistent. With the help of our family friend, Dr. Amish, who treated Abhi and supervised the transplant, we came back to see you."

Abhi's lips began to mutter, "Ro math gudiya (Doll, don't cry)," repeating the words in a weak voice. His body trembled as he watched her cry. Prashanth tried to comfort his son by placing a hand on his shoulder. Abhi pushed him away and continued to repeat the words.

Madhu was shocked to hear the voice and the words. She stopped crying immediately, her sobbing cheeks looking at Abhi with wide-eyed disbelief. "Gudiya" was a secret nickname Krishna had given her. How could this boy know it?

Abhi pushed his dad away and approached Madhu, taking her hands in his. He pulled her close to him and kissed her lips. Madhu seemed frozen, lost in a trance, kneeling on the floor. The doctor, Prashanth, and his wife looked at them in disbelief.

For the next two minutes, no one dared to utter a word. Abhi, shorter than Madhu, pulled her down to sit on the floor, while Madhu's mind was haunted by questions.

"Gudiya, mein aapko chodke kaise jaa sakta hoon, aapne humare liye pariwar aur gaon chodaa hain. Mein aapki kushi chahta hoon, aapko dhukh pahunchaana nahi. Uss din aap se milne, mein jaldbaazi mein gaadi chala raha tha, aur achanak yeh hadsaa hua… mujhe yaad hai, mera haath mobile phone tak gaya, aur aap ko call karne ki koshish ki maine, uske baad, kaha dum nikla, kaha jaan nikli – mujhe pata hi nahi chala".

"Jab mera dil iss bache ke sharir mein dhadakne laga – aap se milne ki aur aap ko dekhne ki kwaaish mein, yeh chaar mahinee beetgaye, mein aur nahi seh sakta tha. Gudiya, aapki khaatir meine jo hamare ghar ki taiyaari ki thi, uske paise yeh Prashanth saab dedenge. Kyon ki mera dil unke iss bache mein dhadak raha hai."

("Angel, I always loved you from the bottom of my heart. You left your family and our village for my sake. My intention is always to keep you happy. Even that day, I was trying to come to you with a good news and this accident happened. Even the conscious last minute after that hapless accident, my hand tried to reach the phone to call you. Don't know when did my eyes closed, my breath stopped forever. But when I woke up again, I took breath with my heart in this boy's body. My heart found a place in this boy. Angel, Mr. Prashanth and family will help me fulfill my lifetime dream of giving you a beautiful house, clearing all the debts. You have to trust me for this. Your eyes should shower tears of joy, but not of pain from now on. I have been waiting for this moment to see you and meet you for the last 4 months.")

"Ab se aapko koi taklif nahi hogi, mera bharosa kariye"

"Abhi's voice choked with deep emotions. So is everyone's in the room. Madhu managed to say this looking at Krishna in Abhi." Kisna, hum kaise jee paayenge? " (How can I live without you, Kisna?)"

Abhi stood up and walked towards Prashant, asking the bag of money to give her. Abhi started stepping out of the room with teary eyes. He paused at the door and turned towards Madhu and told," Gudiya, mera kaam abhi khatam nahi hua. Uss din aapke pitaaji ka call aya tha mujhe, woh aapse milna chahte hai – ye good news bhi aapko batani thi." Khair, ab mein wohi jaa raha hoon, apne gaon. Mein waha jake ye jarur karunga ki aap ko aapke mata pita se milwa doon".

(Angel, my job is not yet done. The good news I wanted to share is that day your father called me on the mobile and expressed her wish to see you. I wanted to tell you and wish to enjoy that happiness in your eyes. Nevertheless, I will go to our town and make sure that your parents come to you and take care of you)

Jiss din ye ho jayega, uss din se mera dil puri tarah se iss bache ka ho jayega. Usey bhi to apni zindagi jeeni hai. Par mein and meri yaadein hamesha aapke sath rahengi!

(Heart will be of Abhi's from then. After all, he has to live his life, that God has given him)

IN THEIR SHOES

"Mamma, Mamma," the little one shouted at the top of her lungs. Mamma was puzzled by her panicked tone. A usually calm girl, the little one's frantic cries confused her.

"Mamma, Mamma," the little one gasped, her voice heavy. Mamma tried to calm her down, saying, "Angel, I'm at work. We have a rule at home: no disturbing Mamma unless it's urgent. Remember that?" Mamma patiently explained, trying to get the little one to speak clearly.

"Mamma, it's urgent. They're here again," the little one said, her voice filled with fear. Mamma and her family were terrified. In fact, the entire colony was scared.

Mamma was momentarily speechless, confused. "Oh no, that shouldn't happen," she muttered. Before she could ask for more details, the little one started shouting again.

"Mamma, you have to come here quickly and get all our aunts. Papa is scared. As I'm talking, he's shivering and won't come out of the room."

"I know that man," Mamma murmured to herself.

"Look, baby, I'll be there as soon as I can. Meanwhile, promise me you won't step outside. By the way, did you check how many of them there are?" Mamma waited for the little one's reply.

"Two people, Mamma, and a little one too. They've been watching our houses for the last hour. Now one of them left to get more help, I think," the little one said.

"Look, angel, you have to hang up. I'll be there in a minute," Mamma said, disconnecting the call.

Mamma stepped out of her workplace, her mind racing with questions. "This is the seventh house we've built in the last few weeks. I hope everything is okay. They come and loot us, destroy our lives, scare us away, and even kill us. This time, I won't let that happen. This is our home, and I'll fight for it," she told herself, her voice loud enough for the women around her to hear.

The situation in the colony was becoming increasingly terrifying by the minute.

Little Angel looked out the window from her room, her eyes filled with fear. Ten feet away, she saw two men and a little boy approaching with sticks of fire and heavy clubs, ready to attack.

The little boy was excited to join the attack but was being warned by the taller, heavier man to stay away. But the little boy was too stubborn and wouldn't budge. "He's just like me," the little one thought.

A moment of childlike imagination turned into gloom as she continued to watch for her Mamma.

"Chottu, you go from that side and set fire to the corner. We have to drive them out. Look, it's already evening. We need to get this done before it gets too dark," the tall man ordered the other.

"Give me one stick, Dad. I'll scare them away too," the excited little one said, reaching for the man's stick.

"No!!!" the man thundered, pushing the little one away. "You'll do it next time, not now. Let me focus on this."

No one in the colony dared to step outside. They were all waiting for their leader, Mamma, and her team. Everyone had lost hope in their homes and most of them, in their lives. As they prayed to God for help, the two men began to set the colony on fire.

Just then, out of nowhere, Mamma arrived!

It wasn't just Mamma. Thousands of her followers stormed the two men from all sides.

"Attack!" Mamma shouted, and the army of women charged at the two men. Terrified, the men tried to run away from the colony but forgot about the little boy.

The Mamma and her army chased the men for twenty yards, but the men managed to evade the attack. However, the boy got caught in the crowd.

The tall man started running back towards the colony, but the other man stopped and threw a stick of fire towards the army.

Mamma's army retreated, leaving the boy injured on the floor.

The little one watched this near-war from her window, her eyes wide open. While she was happy and proud of her brave Mamma, she also felt sad and teary-eyed at the sight of the wounded boy. He wasn't moving.

"God, please take him away. Help him," the little angel prayed.

Just then, Mamma called everyone in the colony to gather. In a matter of minutes, everyone followed her orders and joined her as she began to address them.

"Fellows, we saved our homes today. You all did a great job. With your bravery and trust in my abilities, we saved our hard work, our little ones, our homes, and our food. But this is just the end of one battle. The bad news is, they will be back tomorrow, with even more force. They are filled with vengeance and want to destroy everything. I instruct you all to leave the place as soon as possible. I, as the leader, and my army will stay back and resist their fight until the end. If we secure this beautiful colony, we will bring you back here."

"No more discussions or questions. This is final," Mamma shouted.

The little one looked at her Mamma and started walking towards her room. "Mamma, I want to stay with you," she said softly.

The next day, the newspaper reported, "Tragedy in Kishanpur SEZ land clearing. Two injured and a six-year-old dead in attack by honey bees."

TO CHICHU WITH LOVE

This isn't a letter I should be writing addressing to you. In fact, I shouldn't be addressing it to anyone at all. But today, there's no other choice.

Chichu, you're almost 25 years younger than me, and you call me Dad. But the age difference and the complexities of a father-son relationship have never mattered to us. The secret is, every time I look at you, I see myself growing up all over again. Your smile, your eyes, your adventurous spirit, your silly faces - everything about you reminds me of myself. You are incredibly precious to me, Chichu.

As I write this, my hands tremble, my heart feels heavy, and tears well up in my eyes uncontrollably. Still, I gather the last of my strength to write this.

The next few words are crucial. Please read them carefully.

I was planning to end my life today. To leave this world. To leave you, your mother, everyone...

I know this comes as a heavy burden for you, especially at your young age of eleven. You might want to hit me for doing this and leaving you all behind in difficult times, but trust me, I saw no other way out.

Like everyone else, I wasn't born to just survive. I always imagined myself achieving fame, pushing boundaries. I believed I was an artist, an explorer of the world through writing, not someone confined to society's pre-defined professions.

My father began judging me for this belief from a young age. He wanted me to choose a safe, predictable path. My path was different, something he never understood. I think my failures began there.

I still remember that late-night dinner conversation with my father, while Mom sat in silence. I had just failed my Plus Two exams, the penalty for spending late nights writing scripts for the local theater group.

"What do you want to be?" he demanded.

"Papa," I said, "I want to be the nation's best scriptwriter and director. I want to make films that touch the soul of the Indian audience, while still being entertaining. I can't fit into the predictable cycle of careers and jobs. I'm different." I'm not sure how I mustered the courage to say it. Usually, I was terrified of him when he yelled.

"And how will your madness feed the family?" he simply asked.

"Papa, if I become successful, I'll be a millionaire and famous. It's wealth we, as a working middle-class family, can only dream of!"

"WHAT IF YOU FAIL!?"

This wasn't the first rejection I got from him, but that day, his tone instilled a small fear in my heart. That fear stayed with me, grew with me, ever since.

My worst nightmare of being a failure became my reality. Ten years of struggle, writing hundreds of scripts, working as a spot boy, an assistant director, and taking on all sorts of menial jobs - my dream of becoming a director remained unfulfilled.

After that dinner fight, I left home to pursue my journey. Similar confrontations followed every few weeks.

Your mother is a strong, sensible woman. Despite my failures as a husband and a breadwinner, she picked up the slack. Sensing impending hardship, she got a job and took care of us all.

Perhaps Dad was right about my future - that I wouldn't survive on my own. So, he brought a responsible and sensible daughter-in-law into the family.

Luck was never on my side, Chichu. Therefore, I feel I don't deserve this life anymore.

I always visualized myself as a successful writer and filmmaker, an inspiration in my field. However, at this point in my life, with nothing to show for myself, I sometimes dare not look in the mirror. I feel ashamed.

I muster all my courage for what I'm about to do now.

As I write this letter, I sit across from your bed. Your innocent face is turned towards me, your tiny hands tucked under your cheek, a peaceful smile on your lips.

When you read this, when your mother and my father learn of my death, there will be a period of sadness, a void. But you will all survive. My presence didn't make a huge difference, and neither will my absence.

Here's one piece of advice for you, my dear Chichu - always seek advice from your loved ones while following your dreams. And always know that your dad loves you unconditionally.

Be brave, my son.

Love and kisses,

Papa, Aditya

Ronit's eyes glistened with tears as he folded the letter and tucked it into his pocket. The entire auditorium fell silent. Minutes before filled with excited cheers and the frenzy of hundreds of audience members, the hall was now enveloped in a hush.

"So Ronit, quite a burden you've kept with yourself," the anchor managed to speak, breaking the silence. The entire hall erupted in applause.

A hand rested on Ronit's shoulder, turning him around. He looked up to see Aditya, his father, who embraced him. The audience stood and clapped.

"There you go, ladies and gentlemen," the anchor announced. "Mr. Aditya, the iconic director of our times, a proud father to a great son, and the recipient of the Best Director award for this year's Star Glitz Awards."

Celebrities took to the stage to present the award.

"Now, if you'll allow me," Aditya said, "I'd like to receive this award from this fine gentleman, my son - Ronit."

"Ronit, Ronit, Ronit!" the auditorium echoed with his name as Aditya received his fourth award in his career.

"How did Aditya survive his suicide phase? What happened that day when he left home?" questions swirled in everyone's minds.

As Aditya approached the podium to speak, everyone fell silent.

"This award means a lot to me," he began. "More than that, this life means a lot to me. Eleven years ago, on the day I wrote that letter and left home, I had to walk at least 25 kilometers to reach the suicide point. I had no money in my pocket, so I carried all my writing materials with me. I was ready to end it all.

As I walked, drenched in sweat and barefoot, a stranger jogging past noticed me and approached me impatiently.

'So you won't leave me alone, will you? How many times do I have to tell you not to follow me, stalk me at my home and my office?' he scolded me.

He was Dinesh Banerjee, one of the most successful and top-notch producers in Bollywood.

Suddenly, I don't know how, I found the courage to speak. I had nothing to lose, so I gave my best pitch in that moment.

'Ganesh ji,' I said, 'if you have the energy to say no and push me away, you should have the patience to listen to my story.'

I don't know what went through his mind, but there were no assistants or PAs around to shoo me away. He listened to me. He sat on a bench on the sidewalk and asked me to tell him my story. And the rest, as they say, is history."

"That evening when I came home, Ronit just looked at me," Aditya continued. "The atmosphere was normal. Ronit didn't tell anyone that day. He didn't share this until now. I was surprised that he kept the letter with him."

Aditya, once a man on the brink of despair, was now the country's successful director, a great father to a great son.

THE STORY UNTOLD – PART I

Just as I was falling asleep, my phone rang. I disconnected the first time, but the phone went ringing again in a minute. I forced myself to open my eyes partially, to see Dad displayed on the screen. Irritated, I rubbed my eyes to get rid of the leftover sleep, picking up the call.

"What, Papaji! You know that I come from late night shift. Let's talk in the morning, Papa," I was almost furious.

"Beta, you have to come to Sri Lakshmi Charity Hospital in MG Nagar, right away."

That's not dad, my mind was racing with thoughts.

"Beta, your dad was admitted here because of severe chest pain. He's in the ICU."

God knew only the pace, how did I reach my car and to the hospital in the next 15 minutes, 45 km away! Just as I reached the reception to find out the way to the ICU, I spotted dad's friend, Vasu Rao walking down the hall towards me.

I was searching for minute expressions of sadness or any bad news he was about to reveal. I was praying to God at the same time.

He came closer with a relief on his face. "Dad is fine, just a mild heart stroke. Let's go see him."

A load of some 100 tons was lifted away from my heart as I followed him to the ICU.

Dad was on the bed, seemed weak, but was responding to the doctor's questions normally. I was waiting for the doc and medical crew to clear the space. Just as they left, me and Mr. Vasu Rao reached dad.

"Dad, how did this happen? Told you, not to take any more tensions?"

"Krishna," my dad replied slowly, taking a deep breath, as me and Mr. Rao were waiting for his reply.

"You might not believe what I will say now, but trust me, the incident happened a while ago, but yes, I am the witness of what my eyes saw and my eyes are the witness for what I saw."

"What is the time now?" Dad asked.

"2:15," me and Mr. Rao, both replied.

"I started from the late night meeting at 11:45. The route from MG Road to our home takes a solid 1.5 hours, so I took a short cut, which I thought it would cut 30 minutes. I was sleepy, but was fully alert with music on in the car. Just as I got into the main road from the corner of Old Ganesh Temple, the road is a free-way, so I picked the top gear.

After a 15-minute drive on the road, I stopped at a corner to pee, had a smoke, and slowly started again. This time no music on and kept my window open for some nature's air.

A continuously ringing cycle bell was disturbing my focus on the road. This is abnormal, the sound of the bell is louder than a normal bell. I agree that the sound will be more clear on an empty road and a night, but this is different.

I looked at the cycle and rider of it through the rearview mirror. It is a 15-year-old, with a uniform on and a cap. The uniform is of a store or a hotel. He is full of sweat, but his eyes are wide open, so that he can focus on the road amidst the bright lights of the heavy vehicles coming from the opposite direction.

Just as I give him the space to go forward, an SUV ridiculously hit him from behind, trying to take over and moved forward in a whisk of a second. The next moment, the boy and the cycle crashed under my car, as the boy lost control and my car got over him. I could feel the crush of his bones underneath my car.

I applied sudden breaks and the car stopped at the divider, narrowly hitting the edges of it. I hit my head on the steering wheel as I rubbed my head, trying to get out of the car. What I witnessed is the horror of my life, the boy stood up without any scratches on the body, hurriedly collected the money, which was spread on the road, from his pocket, picked up his cycle, came to me, and shouted on my face, 'Looks like all of you will never allow this Chintu to cross this road and go home.'

His eyes turned blood red and gave an intense look and disappeared from the road.

I was shocked and numb all through this time, with my eyes wide open. With sweat all over the body, I was gone unconscious. When I woke up, I am here."

Dad closed his eyes, while me and Mr. Rao stood there for the next 5 minutes in utter disbelief. While I am sort of guys who don't believe in the existence of spirits and ghosts, I cannot rule out my dad's experience too.

Two days later, my dad was sent home and doctors instructed for a bed rest for a couple more days. I decided to take leave and take care of him, along with mom.

Life is back on track till when I read that article in the Sunday Magazine.

THE HAUNTING ROAD OF MG HIGHWAY.

As I read through the story, I understood that MG Highway, on any given day is a busy road, with vehicles from both sides, not much of the civilian place around, as it is surrounded by barren lands. Till 1 year before, there used to be night hawkers selling apples or China toys at the main signals till midnight, till Chintu, the boy ghost started haunting that road.

As the clock strikes 12:15 midnight, this ghost appears from nowhere on a cycle, with a jet speed, trying to overtake the vehicles, while ringing the cycle bell. The shocking part is, the ghost either falls under the vehicle, gets crushed or hits the divider, due to cars or vehicles not giving it the way to move forward. As the ghost rises without any scratches, it disappears in front of their eyes. Most of the witnesses succumbed to severe shocks, heart strokes, or the worst of it, paralysis.

Till now, 11 witnesses or the victims have shared the same experience. The astonishing part is, all of these incidents happened either on the 5th or 10th of any given month.

I folded the paper and kept it on the table and went into a deep thought. For the first time, I started believing in the existence of ghosts and I believe this ghost called Chintu is doing so for a strong reason.

Why does he subject himself to get himself killed, every time?

Why only on the 5th or 10th of any month?

Who is this Chintu?

My mind started asking me more questions as I looked at the calendar for the nearest 5th or 10th.

10th March, 3 days to go!

"Let's find this Chintu," I told myself as I woke up to get ready for the office.

THE STORY UNTOLD – PART II

The signal turned green, and I accelerated, relishing the smooth sound of the new tires on the road. The adrenaline rush was exhilarating as I sped down the empty highway. The speedometer reached 130!

Lost in the thrill of speed but focused on the road ahead, I glanced out my right window. To my horror, Chintu was on his cycle, racing alongside my car, his head turned towards me. I couldn't see his face clearly, just a dark shadow.

Shocked, I tried to slow down. The cycle hit my car, and I felt his face strike the window. Through the darkness, I saw his bloodshot eyes staring at me, as if saying, "Won't you allow Chintu to cross this road?"

My heart pounded, and my body froze in shock. I opened my eyes and jumped out of bed, as if dodging an attack.

"I'm dreaming! This scary dream and that scarier Chintu left me with a severe headache."

For the last two days, the memories of this incident hadn't faded. It seemed I had to solve this.

March 10th. I didn't know why I was chasing something that might not exist. It could be a hallucination. But I had never seen my dad so fragile after this incident.

When you witness the unknown, your senses are challenged. Suddenly, you feel less powerful, controlled by beyond-life phenomena. I started praying to God for strength.

I told my friend about this. He simply advised me not to chase the dark. He explained that ghosts or spirits like that carry a curse, and chasing them could risk your life and bring that curse upon you.

His explanation was frightening indeed!

Time 3 PM. I tried to sleep all morning and afternoon to stay focused. I shouldn't miss a bit of what might happen today. I wasn't sure I would find what I was searching for, but the only question in my mind was, "Who is Chintu?"

I parked my car near the Old Ganesh Temple. The usually busy junction was empty today. Surprised, I walked along the pavement, talking to a few locals. I found out that the head of the local trade merchants had passed away, so the shops were closed.

Shit! The local shopkeepers were the first source of information on this road. I missed them. As I started walking down the road, a man in his late 50s, wearing a shabby lungi and kurta, limped towards me, asking for 50 rupees.

I rejected him and kept walking. He followed me. I found an old man sitting near the wall, enjoying his sutta. I went to him, gave him 10 rupees, and started asking about Chintu. He looked at me with blank eyes and said, "Chintuji? I am a big fan of him. I liked his first movie 'Bobby.' Dimple is so beautiful in the movie. I also liked him in Chandini and Deewana. Bol Radha Bol is good too." He kept talking and singing Chintuji's (Rishi Kapoor's) songs one after the other.

I decided to run as soon as possible from there. I stopped at a tree for shade, but when I looked back, the man who had been following me for the last hour was still there. I went to him and gave him 50 rupees. He looked at the note on both sides and kept it in his pocket. "You are asking for Chintu. I know about him."

He started walking, and I followed him, asking various questions. What, where, how...

He didn't open his mouth until we reached the deserted highway. It looked like 10 km from where I had parked the car. I checked my watch - 7 PM.

OMG! Time just flew. I had been outside for the last 4 hours.

The man sat on a bench, looking at the road.

"Jitesh Govardhan, alias Chintu, came to the city with his father and two sisters for labor work. Kashiram, his father, was once a decent farmer in his hometown but was cheated by his own friends and partners. He had to leave his town for survival. The embarrassment left him with a paralysis attack, which made him partially handicapped.

The burden fell on Chintu, who had passed his Grade 10th with distinction. He had dreams of further studies, but they were all crushed by his current responsibilities. Right now, he had to work his ass off to earn some bread for the family.

For almost 4 days, Chintu and his sisters had to beg for food to feed his father. It was the most humiliating situation for him, who had a great upbringing by his dad in the village.

He decided to work. Daily jobs were not guaranteed. A distant relative who was working in the city advised him to get a monthly-paying job.

He got a job in the MPM Mall in MG Road, the most elusive mall of the city. Chintu was young and attractive but didn't have proper clothes to wear for work in a big mall. The greedy team lead traded his first month's salary for 4 T-shirts and pants and a worn-out cycle.

No first month salary for him. On top of that, he had to travel 35 km to the mall from his so-called home.

He waited for another 15 days, with hardly 100 rupees in his pocket. He went to his team lead in the mobile shop he worked in and asked for an advance.

That guy treated him like shit and threatened to fire him if he asked for an advance again. Poor Chintu, he compromised with the pain, tight under his lip.

The first week of the month arrived. Chintu was relieved that he could finally feel the touch of currency, his hard-earned money. At last, they could buy a stove to make food instead of begging or waiting at the community center. He could take his dad to the doctor.

With all the excitement in his heart and mind, he called the mobile phone of his landlord to give the call to his dad. He reluctantly took the phone to his dad.

Whatever he talked on the phone brought a smile to his dad's face that day.

Before disconnecting the call, Chintu said that he would be coming early with biryani, his dad's favorite dish, for his sisters. They would all have a party.

The clock struck 9:30 PM, and the shop was closing in 30 minutes. Chintu didn't get his salary. He went to the team lead for it. He made him wait till 11:30 PM that night. He made him close the shop, lock it, and get liquor for him and his seniors for their after-hours party. As they finished their drinking session, the team lead gave him his salary.

Chintu pushed the currency into his pocket without even counting it and started rushing on the cycle. He started crying and cursing himself on the way for not being able to buy fresh food for his family, for missing their first-ever party on the salary. Now, all he wanted was to rush home faster and show them the money, which gave a hope for a better tomorrow.

Chintu was on the highway, already out of energy but looking at the empty road, he gathered all the energy to pace forward on the cycle. His energy was almost drained from eating only once a day. His eyes were on the dirty street ahead, where home lay. As he almost reached the turn, he wanted to cross the road, giving the hand signal. A sports car, which was going at 130 km/h, came from nowhere and hit him from behind without stopping.

Chintu was thrown into the air and hit the road. The cycle was smashed into pieces. His head hit the road, and in no time, the grey road turned red with his blood. Severely wounded, Chintu tried to crawl and cross the road, saying, 'I have to go home. I have to meet my dad and tell him that we have hope to live.'

Vehicles just passed by him, not stopping to help him at all. Humanity works only during the day.

He was dead after a few minutes.

When his body was taken home, there was silence around. It seemed the pain had become a pleasure for them. His dad prayed to God loudly, when he was about to cremate.

'Thank God for taking Chintu from the jungle of wild animals. We just don't have the guts to follow him.' He collapsed.

Chintu died, but his intention to feed his family didn't. He had been trying to come home since then, but this civilian world was scared, as he was a ghost!

Nevertheless, he would try again today."

My eyes were full of tears. I didn't have a word to say. I held my head and sat on the bench beside, silent for a few minutes.

"Chintu had a right to live in this world, like all of us. Is there a way that I can reach his family and help them on Chintu's behalf?"

There was no reply from the man. I raised my head to look at him.

The man was gone. I searched for him around but in vain.

"Who was that man? His dad, the landlord, the neighbor, who knew about Chintu?

"Who is that man? His dad, the landlord, the neighbor, who knew about Chintu?"

Before my mind started searching for answers to these questions, I closed my eyes and wholeheartedly prayed to God, "May Chintu's soul rest in peace."

THERE IS ALWAYS A FIRST TIME

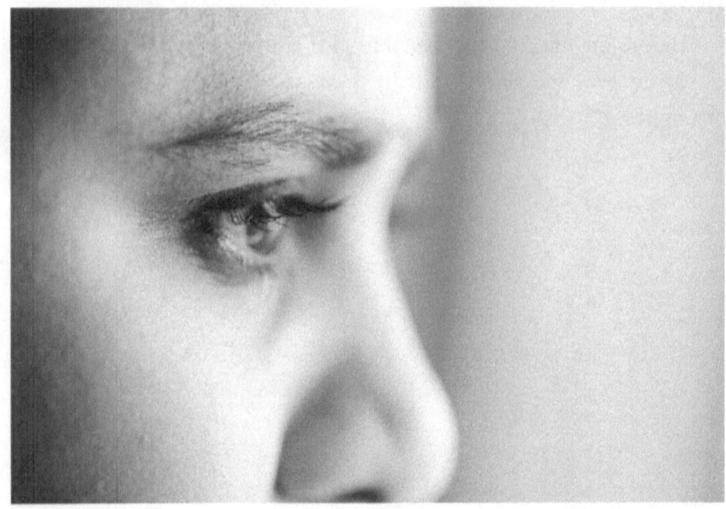

24-year-old Tina was anxiously waiting outside the room. The clock struck 7:30 PM. Lost in her nervousness and anxiety, Tina suddenly stood up from her chair, looking at the clock and starting to walk in the corridor. Her beautiful face was filled with drops of sweat, and her hands were slightly shivering.

A perfect girl, that's what Tina's friends called her. Whether it was her stunning physique or the cool attitude she carried naturally, she had an X factor.

Life was a normal ride until two days before that penthouse party, when Tina was enjoying with her friends over a beer and received a call.

A strong hand on her shoulders brought her back to the present. A heavily built man in his mid-30s, with well-oiled hair and a protruding belly, stood beside her. Tina stood up and gave him a nervous glance. That glance made him even more conscious, as if she were scanning him inside out. He started adjusting his jeans over his pot belly and asked her to follow him into the adjacent room.

Tina started walking behind him, her eyes and fingers on her phone, trying to end some chat conversations on her WhatsApp.

"First time for you?" the man asked her without turning back.

"Hmm... well... yes, I tried to do this before, but didn't have the guts," she said slowly.

He took her into a room with a bed in the center. Silence filled the room. Tina's anxiety grew fourfold, and she could hear her heart pounding in the eerie quiet.

The man started ogling at her, his eyes lingering on her voluptuous chest for a moment, his mouth wide open. Tina became conscious and turned her back, going to the corner.

She leaned over the wall, resting on her hands, and started talking to herself. "Baby, you are a killer! You can do this... I know this is the first time. But anything has a first time, and you will do it."

"You will do it. You will do it. You will do it. Tina is a rock star. You can do it." Her self-assurance and motivation lasted for the next two minutes.

"Guess this is your first time. Fear is written all over," the man winked at her. "Don't worry, all you have to do is cooperate with me. Let me do this softly, so there is no pain for you," the man said firmly and reassuringly.

Tina slowly walked towards the bed and sat on it.

"Do I have to change?" Tina asked slowly.

The man started laughing loudly, busy setting some things around. "No need, you just lay down and close your eyes. I will make it quick."

She got onto the bed, her fists clenched tightly.

"Quick, quick, quick - how quick will it be?" A storm of questions flooded her mind and slowly appeared on her face.

The man came slowly to her and bent over her. "Trust me, this will be painless and quick. Your first time will be smooth, thanks to my experience."

"How many times have you done this till now?" Tina asked him curiously.

He closed his eyes and got into a counting mode. "69 to be precise, till now!"

"Most of them are first-timers."

He slowly reached for her hand, held it tightly, and looked into her eyes.

Tina was already drowned in utmost fear as the man came closer to her. Her breath quickened as he slowly inserted it into her.

Tina's eyes widened with pain as she looked up at the ceiling for a moment. The pain shot through her nerves in no time.

A minute later, the pain slowly gave way to an inexplicable pleasurable feeling as the fluid finds its way. She could feel a different kind of sensation, something she had never experienced in her whole life.

"Oh god! This is far more exciting than a drug."

As the man continued, she slowly closed her eyes and enjoyed the process.

"Told you it would be quick," the man whispered in her ear slightly louder. That brought Tina back to her senses. She looked at him. He was near the washbasin, cleaning his hands and face.

She woke up and sat on the bed.

"Yeah, I did it!!!" Tina wanted to shout, but she enjoyed the moment from inside and kept a blank expression on her face.

She slowly tried to get off the bed, as the man came and helped her.

"How about next time?" the man winked at her. "Not now though, after three months."

As Tina slowly walked out of the room, her heart filled with a sense of pride for doing it for the first time.

As she came into the corridor, a young couple came to her and hugged her with gratitude, their eyes filled with tears.

Rohit and Meera, Tina's besties, looked at this from a distance.

"Tina deserves a treat this evening. She has saved a child's life by donating blood. Look how happy the couple is," Rohit said.

"That's true, she might have overcome her fear of donating blood. I knew her spending two sleepless nights to take this action," Meera added.

As Tina walked towards them, both went to her, shouting, "So proud of you, baby!" and hugged her.

Tina's eyes were filled with tears. Tears of joy, pride for overcoming her fear, and for saving a life!

THAT NIGHT.......

"Sipping on rosé, sipping on sun, feeling so lazy – This is how we do... umm... sipping yeah... This is how we do," Riya shouted, her voice echoing through the boutique.

Mala approached her, pulling off her headphones. "Stop it, will you? Your singing is terrible, and English songs, of all things! What happened to Sunidhi Chauhan? You're more like Kate Perry these days. Kisko impress karna hai?"

Riya pushed Mala away and walked to the table. "Stop touching my cups, you bitch" she snapped. "And by the way, this isn't nakhra huh; this is who I am. How long have you known me? Six months? Before this, I was in Mumbai and in Delhi before that. Mehra Seth was so impressed he got me from his uncle's place."

"Wherever you came from, you're here now, in this town with us Nautanki Rani and that makes us equals," Dolly shouted from upstairs.

Riya turned furious and walked away, sitting in a chair opposite the mirror. Her mood slowly calmed as she looked at the handsome man, her crush in the aisle standing with his friend, who winked at her. Riya blushed.

Mala noticed this and rushed towards Riya, pushing herself against her. She started whispering in her ear, "My god! All this natak and nautanki for him, na, Riya? Bolo bolo..."

Riya stepped away from Mala, signaling her to be quiet. She took Mala to a corner and whispered, "Are you…..? Do you want Dolly and her gang to know this? She'll ruin everything. Mala, I'm scared to propose to him yaar, but I'm really attracted to him and deeply in love Tonight's the night I tell him how I feel. Naya maal is arriving tomorrow. A girl from London is coming. Firang hai, koi bhi chance nahi chodegi aur wo to meri taraf dekhega bhi nahi. Kuch to karo jaan, please doo something," Riya pleaded.

Mala leaned against the wall, took a deep breath, and said, "But upstairs, that extra Size Zandu Lal is madly in love with you, and you know that. He's really sincere about you, baby. You're focusing too much on muscles and looks. You're missing out on a golden heart who cares for you." Mala was looking upstairs at the overweight man who was hiding behind the pillar and looking at Riya with adoration in his both eyes.

Arey….. yeh mera dil hain ya koi Dharamshaala, ki anyone knocks and comes in, eats me and leaves shit? Who asked him to like me. "I've never even looked at him, let alone talked to him. Forget it, sweetheart. One more heart has to break, I can't help it. Let it happen this evening.

Zandu Lal's eyes were filled with tears. His thick glasses blurred with moisture.

Riya didn't care. Her chest heaved, and her heart pounded as she turned to look at the man she admired.

Mala slowly watched Zandu Lal cry. Then she turned to Riya, patted her shoulder, wished her luck, and pushed her toward the man.

Riya hesitated and stepped forward, but then quickly turned back to the mirror to do a quick touch-up. After a few minutes, she took a deep breath and walked toward him.

He was sitting comfortably in the chair, his right arm resting on his friend's shoulder. They were talking closely.

"He's talking about me, for sure," Riya thought to herself.

She walked toward him and sat down in an empty chair next to him. He and his friend were immediately aware of her presence.

There was silence for a few minutes. Riya and the Man were too nervous to speak.

Mala was watching them keenly from a distance. She was praying, a bit loudly, "Bhagwanji please, Riya ki line clear ho gayi, to mujhe bhi uska dost mil jayega. God, please help me."

Mala kept praying for the next 5 minutes with closed eyes. Suddenly, she felt a hard tap on her back. She turned to see Riya crying, her eyes red and her mascara smeared all over her face.

"F****** A******le, chutiya, kya socha kya usne mere baare mein?" she started cursing, using every swear word she knew. Mala was confused for a moment, but then regained her composure.

"Arey hua kya? Tell me the good news first, ye galiya baadme dena", Mala said.

"What good news do you want to hear? Tell me, Mala, tell me. You'll be shocked when you hear this," Riya whispered in Mala's ear.

"Arey baba, he's gay, and they're both in love. They met in Delhi and want to get married. They're looking at me, the fool, for help because they think my word goes here" exclaimed Riya disappointed.

"Oh my god!", Mala fainted. Dolly and her gang burst into loud laughter. They made fun of Riya, "Arey Priya dekho, milne gayi thi saiyya ko aur mil gaya bhaiya".

The rest of the night was filled with Dolly and her friends' laughter at Riya and Mala's expense. Meanwhile, Zandu Lal watched from upstairs with a glimmer of hope.

The next morning.................

Fat Chatterjee entered the hall to see the chaos caused by Riya and Dolly.

"What's going on? Chintu, come quickly and take these girls to the corner. Mr. Seth will be here any minute," Chatterjee said, trying to pull Dolly away.

"Why are all these mannequins scattered throughout the hall? What is this mess?" an angry voice came from behind. Mehra Seth, a 51-year-old man, stood in the center of the hall with his iPhone in his right hand.

"You all have only 30 minutes to take all these mannequins and throw them into the storeroom. We have a new batch of ladies' wear arriving from Shangai. The container arrived yesterday, and they might come to our store anytime. How long can we keep selling this old stuff? Get rid of it before I decide to burn it all down," he ordered.

The staff quickly gathered all the mannequins, Dolly and her friends, Mala, and Riya, and threw them into the dark hall behind the garment store, locking the door behind them.

For the first time, Zandu Lal dared to hold Riya's hand.

BEYOND BORDERS

"I was born to fly. That's what my parents say. They told me so in a language I could understand when I was a baby, trying to open my tiny eyes and see this vast world. Born in the lap of Mother Nature, I had nothing to complain about, with doting parents and a caring community. Until one fine day, when my dad came to me and said, 'Son, it's time for you to explore the world and help our community.'

From that day, I became a world traveler – able to cross borders without any passports or visas. You might be thinking I'm the son of the world's most powerful leader or a peacemaker (go ahead and guess!).

Previous generations of my community perceived the world as four directions – East, West, North, and South. Not that they were ignorant, but that limited knowledge was self-sufficient for them. As time changed and the human population grew, the world became divided, and we had to understand and learn geography. We had to understand the world – by its countries, cities, counties, etc.

My great grandfather, who still lives with us, mocks the world's division into tiny ice blocks like a mega glacier. 'Beware, kiddo – the city you visited last year might not be on the map today,' he warns.

'True,' my father added, reminiscing about his travels around the world. 'Who could imagine the mighty Soviet Union – our neighboring land, a favorite vacation spot in summers – being broken into seventeen nations?'

As I traveled across nations, met different people, and witnessed different lifestyles, one thing became clear: A person living in a cosmopolitan city in the USA has nothing in common with a person living in a small village in India. They don't even care about each other as fellow human beings.

The truth is, in this world of various countries, one country of people is just a piece of news to the other – good or bad. Nothing more, nothing less! Thanks to the media-dominated world, news is less emotional and more factual. That way, you move on with your life.

My private jet needs no fuel, no need to stop at airports or take air clearance. (Now your wild guesses might take a wild turn, folks!)

All my family had traveled west, so I thought it was time for me to go south, to Africa. From a world of green woods, snowy mountains, scanty people, and grazing cows in Europe, I was transported to a dying, destitute, hopeless piece of brown land – Africa. I never expected such a shock. All it took was an unpredictable cyclone that hit for four days over the Red Sea, forcing me to divert to Somalia.

Tired and broken, I had no energy to move ahead and had to rest near a village. With one fish I had caught from the sea, I was ready to eat my last supper (I had been without food for the last three nights, thanks to the mother f***ing cyclone!). As I was about to eat the fish, I spotted a nearly dead man begging for a drop of water.

Feeling pity for him, I went to him and dropped the fish into his mouth. Hunger doesn't know taste, I was thinking, as he devoured the fish, even the fins. A minute later, I could see life returning to his eyes.

After that, I swear to god I would never want to step into this sorry part of the world. As I was leaving that region, I overheard a philosopher saying, 'The world is full of terrorism.'

Africa is full of hunger terrorism. The Middle East is full of religious terrorism. The West is full of capitalist terrorism. Is terrorism the new god of this generation? I wondered as I left that country. As I flew into deep clouds, I could see the entire landscape of the sick, hunger-stricken, terror-struck Horn of Africa.

It's not just one country in the entire world where hunger is visibly clear. In Africa, it's more apparent, while in other parts of the world, it's overshadowed by aggressive consumerism and urban architecture – the skyscrapers that almost reach the sky dominate the rag streets filled with hapless and poor souls.

'Don't fly on weekends – starting Friday evening till Sunday night,' my old traveler colleague advised me. I wisely took that advice and stayed low during the next few days.

'Until a few years ago, we were part of nature as much as them. These days, they are nature, and we are the aliens,' my father said during one of the turbulent times.

'True,' I thought now. My mission of finding a safe place for my community was almost getting blurred now, as the world outside was much horrified and controlled.

Crossing one small country of Africa, then the sea, then back to Europe, my six-month journey of exploring a safe place for my community ended. Now I had to face them with a blank face. Thoughts were mushrooming in my mind. Just then, my wings were suddenly crippled, and I was falling down.

I was shot! Before I could think about what had just happened, I hit the ground hard, and all my bones were crushed due to the heavy impact. My eyes, which were wide open in flight, were filled with blood and closing down forever as I saw four men with guns in their hands running toward me, shouting, 'Bitch, it got hit!'

One fat man spat on me, saying, 'How dare the bird of that country cross the border and fly in our country?'

The other guy added, 'Yeah, how dare them to send their national bird, which rules their flags, across the line to fly over our land?'

Before I took my final breath, I understood this: 'I happened to be the national bird of their rival country, and no air or bird of theirs can enter here? So, how am I connected to their rivalry, vengeance, and hatred?'

Oh! I didn't tell you who I am. I'm just a bird on a migration mission. A bird that is nothing compared to your mighty human strength, brilliance, and arrogance. I am no one before you. I might be a dish for your weekend, if my time is bad.

Now before you ask me what kind of bird I am – seagull, hummingbird, woodpecker, or penguin – I am just a bird with two wings – not an African, Asian, Indian, American, Arab, Hindu, or Muslim.

You want to rule this earth, do it, but not at the cost of our nature. Goodbye, forever!"

THE LAST MEET

"Auto!" Latha yelled at the top of her voice. An auto was waiting 5 feet away, and the driver came out and asked, "Madam, yahi hoon mein, itna chillana kaiku?" An old man across the street, two schoolchildren, and two young people sitting at the bakery turned their heads towards her.

Anxious and nervous, Latha wasn't in the mood to check on everyone. She quickly got into the auto and asked the driver to go to Panjagutta.

The driver simply replied, "Nahi jata madam udhar, bahot traffic hai waha." Latha raised her voice and said she would give him double the meter.

He turned back to say something, but looking at her, the driver didn't utter a word. After a minute, the auto started towards the main road. As the auto entered the heavy traffic of Hyderabad, it seemed lost in the ocean of vehicles, and so was Latha, who was already lost in her whirlwind of thoughts.

“Sanjay,” her lips uttered in a voice that only she could hear.

“It’s been 5 years, I haven’t heard from him,” she said to herself.

Ten years before, life was different.

In August 2004, I met him at my college. He was my senior.

In January 2005, I went out with him for coffee for the first time.

“He proposed to me while we were watching ‘Fanaa.’ Until that moment, I was lost in the world of Aamir and Kajol, and from the next minute, I was his.”

“Sanjay is a 6-foot package of surprises. He knows how I think and feel at every moment. He would look into my eyes, hold me tighter, and say, ‘Latha, what are you hiding from me? I know you inside out now.’”

“The man who knew me and my heart so much, why did he have to leave me at the crossroads and leave for his career?” Latha started talking to herself, perhaps more loudly, so the auto driver looked at her from the mirror.

She adjusted herself and was lost in thoughts again. “Latha, my mother has high expectations of me, and before that, anything can wait. And that includes you. The responsibility for building a great life is on both of us, and I’m sure my project in the US will change things in our favor. Trust me. Six more months!”

“But my family had other plans for me, and they were quicker. Three months later, my marriage was arranged to a Bangalore-based techie. Ten days later, I was married. The night before my marriage, he called me. It was a coincidence. When I told him about the marriage, there was silence. Deep silence for the next 15 minutes. I could hear sobbing from the other end, and then the line disconnected.”

“I couldn’t control myself from that moment. I couldn’t express my love for him. Feelings of anger, guilt, and sadness overwhelmed me.”

“Time flew, my family life started with compromise, later love blossomed out of it, and in the next 4 years, our family grew with two little daughters.

I was not a young person anymore. I was a responsible housewife, a loving mother of two daughters, and an obedient daughter-in-law who gave up her job for the family. Everything was going well, until yesterday – the call from Sanjay."

Time – 6:30 PM – the evening traffic in Hyderabad is always a scary thing. Latha started looking at her watch impatiently. She shouted at the driver to go faster. He said in a cool manner, without turning back, "Jaldi hi chala raha madam, auto driver hoon, Superman nahi."

She ignored his words as she looked at the coffee shop where they had gone for the first time.

She couldn't recognize the voice at first. "Latha, this is Sanjay," he said. She went numb for a few minutes on the phone.

"Latha, do you remember me?" Sanjay asked in a low tone, but full of affection. Latha came back to normalcy and replied sarcastically, "Yes, why would I forget you? You were the only Sanjay in my life. I didn't have many." She started crying.

Sanjay tried to comfort her, but she couldn't stop. "Look, I didn't call to bother you like this. For the last time, I want to meet you tomorrow because I'm leaving for Zurich forever the day after tomorrow. I have no one to come back here, Latha, please understand. My mom, dad, and younger brother died in an accident last year." His voice faltered, but he regained his composure and said, "I'm not trying to get back into your otherwise peaceful life. All I want is one last coffee with you, at the place where we met for the first time, tomorrow evening at 7 PM, please."

He immediately disconnected the phone, but Latha couldn't. Deep down, she hadn't forgotten him. She had been yearning to hear his voice. Her mind said no to the proposal, but her heart was in control.

Lost in thoughts, Latha passed the coffee shop where they had met. She immediately asked the driver to take a turn around. The driver did so. Her eyes were searching for Sanjay.

"How will he be now? I always liked his hairstyle. Hope he still has the same style. What should I do when I meet him? Should I hug him, slap him for leaving me like this, or forget the world and be his for the next few minutes? Am I doing wrong?"

The auto stopped exactly opposite the coffee shop on the other side of the road. She looked for a thin, tall man with a beard, a white shirt, and blue jeans, anxiously waiting for her near the parking. He looked at the auto and Latha, and his anxious eyes suddenly turned joyful.

She got out of the auto.

The very happy Sanjay signaled her to come to him. Sanjay started crossing the road, his eyes on Latha. He was so happy at that moment.

In the next second, the unimaginable happened. Latha looked at the scene in utter shock and awe.

Sanjay was hit by an ambulance that was speeding towards the nearby Nijams hospital. The ambulance, with its siren blaring, had lost sight of Sanjay and couldn't avoid him. The van ran over his skull and forcefully stopped at a distance.

Suddenly, the spot was crowded with people, police, and onlookers on the other side of the road.

Latha's eyes widened, and she was paralyzed for a moment. She had lost everything at that moment but couldn't reveal herself.

She asked the driver to start the auto. The driver was puzzled. "But madam, you just arrived."

She was in a trance and couldn't say anything. Her eyes filled with tears. The traffic en route to her home was not that dense, and the auto started cruising towards her destination.

Latha had no time to cry. She started settling herself, trying to be normal, like nothing had happened.

She stepped into her house, and her two little children rushed to her. Latha smiled and said, "Give me 10 minutes, dears. Let me freshen up and fix your dinner."

She locked the bedroom door behind her and got under the shower. As the water showered on her, her eyes cried with it and her heart ached. The burden was heavy and couldn't be easily lifted, as the last sight of Sanjay was still stuck in her mind and heart. But she had to move on...

ANYTHING BUT TEA

Aichi Yamamoto had a wish. A wish that had been hidden for years since he was four. Like any other young male member of his Kishotu tribe, he had to wait until he reached twelve years old to drink his most coveted beverage of his land – tea.

Yes, you heard it right. Tea as a beverage was considered the most prestigious drink for the Kishotu tribe, unlike any other tribes or native lands in Japan. One of the tribe's forefathers was believed to have created a new blend of tea that became famous among the Nipponese and Cantonese regions. When Japan ruled Chinese lands, a lot of exchanges occurred, including cuisines and tea blends, entering Japan. Kishotu tribes had worked in the army and brought the glory of new tea blends into the tribe and the region.

No wonder, tea was considered prestigious, and boys had to turn twelve years old and undergo a public ritual on Full Moon Day to taste it. Drinking tea in the ritual would make Yamamoto a young adult and allow him to enter the public house, the tribe's mini-parliament.

Until then, Yamamoto was not allowed into the kitchen and could only have dinner with his young cousins. But the aroma of tea and the delicious discussions around it made Yamamoto desperate and determined to drink tea by any means.

At night, he dreamed of drinking tea served by beautiful women all around or owning a tea café with people forming long queues outside while he enjoyed his tea alone.

Dream after dream, he felt more and more connected to the magic of tea, but in reality, nothing was moving in his favor.

Yamamoto was now ten years old, still two or three years away from his goal. He had lost interest in the sweets his ugly, fat uncle got him from Tokyo. Homemade desserts tasted sour to him. All he wanted was tea. He was terrified of the punishments he might receive if he was caught drinking it.

He had now decided to ask for it, to demand it!

The time and occasion were set. The Aichi Family was all set to attend the grand marriage reception of their daughter, hosted by the Village head.

Excitement filled the air, along with the fragrances. Children were playing outside the venue, and the elders were sitting in the right wing, enjoying their tea. Yamamoto spotted his grandfather, who loved him so much and pampered him, unlike his father. The young Yamamoto thought he was the best person who could make his wish come true.

He approached his grandfather and held out his hands to hug him. Yamamoto accepted his hug without hesitation.

A few minutes later, the loudness and excitement came to a sudden halt with the grandfather's loud shout at Yamamoto, who had requested a cup of tea in public. The grandfather took it as an insult and asked him to leave the venue immediately.

The young Yamamoto's ego was hurt, and he turned his back on his grandfather and walked towards his mother, who was witnessing the incident in shock. "What happened to this kid?" Lady Aichi wondered.

"I should take him home before his father beats him," she thought and started walking towards him.

What Yamamoto did next shocked everyone. He grabbed a cup of tea ready for serving, sipped it, and threw the glass into the crowd. He pushed the servant when he tried to catch him.

Yamamoto's father slapped him hard, which made him faint.

When he woke up a few hours later, all he could see was fire and smoke. "Thanks to Yamamoto's desperation, all this mess happened. The marriage got canceled because the venue was burned down," someone shouted.

"This is a bad omen. Yamamoto broke the code, which he shouldn't have done in the first place. He should not be drinking tea in this life henceforth. If he drinks, it's bad luck for this region," the village head declared. The village head, an older man, was very frustrated, not only because the marriage was canceled but also because of the immense investment he had made and the damage to his reputation.

Yamamoto shook his head in disbelief. "This old man has decided to ruin my dreams for life. What is this? A vendetta?" he thought.

He had to accept it.

Eleven years passed.

During this period, Yamamoto tried drinking tea by any means, but fate or coincidence had other plans for his deeds. Whenever he attempted to drink tea, there was always an earthquake on the island, a mutiny on the government, or a fire accident.

Yamamoto decided there was a natural connection between these two occurrences. One fine day, he vowed before Buddha that he would never taste tea again in his life.

It was a tough decision for him, but he had to live with it.

Yamamoto got involved in his family business and took over his dad's seat. His determination and focus brought in great revenues even during wartime. The entire region, including the tribe, was proud of him.

"It's time for him to get married," his dad decided. His mom nodded. "But for a change, let's try matches outside our tribe."

His father agreed.

The day came when the family went to see the bride.

Anxiously waiting to see the bride, who they said was the most beautiful girl on the island, Yamamoto was so happy and excited.

His eyes were fixed on the stairs from where the girl would be coming to meet the elders. His focus, breath, everything was on how the first meeting would be.

Would she smile at him? Would she look into his eyes?

A thousand questions stormed his mind, yet he didn't reveal a single one on his face. He felt like his heart was bursting with joy.

Something stuck between him and the stairs. Yamamoto raised his head. The servant with a plate in his hand was trying to offer him something.

He took the glass and sipped it. The taste told him it was tea!

Yamamoto was back to normal but pleasantly enjoyed his first cup of tea in front of the world. His parents and relatives started murmuring and looked worried about the upcoming havoc.

But Yamamoto, who was earlier lost in the girl's dreams, was now lost in his world of tea. He enjoyed every sip of the tea, slowly, artistically. Worth the wait, he thought!

Just as he was about to order another cup, there was a deafening explosion outside. Everyone went numb for a minute, confused about what had happened.

After a few minutes, everyone climbed the nearby hillock to see what had happened. A mushroom-shaped cloud spread for miles in the sky, hundreds of miles away.

No one understood what it was. But from behind, as someone switched on the radio, the news came out: America had attacked the cities of Hiroshima and Nagasaki with atomic bombs some time ago. The cities were totally destroyed, and the vicinity was under severe radiation. Residents were advised to move to safe places.

"I knew some havoc would come when Yamamoto drinks tea, but of this scale!" one relative shouted.

But where was Yamamoto? Everyone looked around. He was not there.

His parents searched for him throughout the town and everywhere. There were no whereabouts.

A rumor spread for years in the region that Yamamoto was the unlucky mascot, and with tea in hand, he became the destruction.

Everyone except his parents felt very happy and rejoiced for Yamamoto's absence.

In 1973, New York, America:

Young Mishito came to work for the first time on Wall Street. For weeks, he hadn't had authentic Japanese food or tea. During lunchtime, he asked his colleagues to show him the best Japanese restaurant.

They talked about one in Manhattan that was considered the best in America.

"What do they offer?" Mishito curiously asked.

Charles, his colleague, coughed and said, "Look! I've never been there, but I heard they're the best. The food is heavenly, it seems."

"And tea?" Mishito asked. "What about that?"

"They offer coffee, not tea! In fact, outside the restaurant, there's a board in bold red letters that says, 'WE OFFER ANYTHING JAPANESE, EXCEPT TEA.' Strange!" Charles said.

Mishito was silent for a minute and suddenly shouted, "Brother Yamamoto!!!!!!!!!!!!!!!!!!!!!!!!!!!!!!"

THE INVITE

Mark lazily opened the letter that had been dropped at his doorstep. The envelope was very old and addressed to the New Regime Football Club. He turned it over to see where it was from. It simply said, "There is nothing like undelivered, when we send an invite."

Quite an attitude, he thought. He went to the director's room, where Bill was busy on a loud phone call. Mark waved the letter in front of his face. Bill put down the phone, took the letter, and told Mark to leave the room. After a minute, he slowly opened the envelope, took out the letter, and began to read it.

As he read, his facial expression changed from surprise to shock to fear. When he finished, he was drenched in sweat. Mark was watching from outside the glass door. He went inside to turn on the air conditioner for Bill. Bill was still in shock. All he could say was, "Assemble the Young Turks team." The Young Turks were the Grade D team of the highly successful New Regime Football Club. Mark left the room puzzled, wondering why Bill, the Big Man of the club, wanted to meet with the rookie team.

Ten minutes later, Bill entered the team room, where the 15-member team, coach, and assistant were waiting. Bill stepped inside, told the coaches to leave the room, and Mark noticed the same fear on Bill's face that he had seen earlier.

Bill opened his mouth, searching for the right words, but acted as if nothing had happened. "Team, this is a life-changing opportunity for all of you here. The oldest club in the world, The Pheonix FC, sent a letter this morning inviting one of our clubs for a late-night match at their club stadium. And I want you to play it; not the senior team."

"Now the time is 4:15 in the evening. Let's keep this a secret. Do not reveal this to anyone. Keep your phones in your lockers and practice until 9."

"When is the match, sir?" young Philippe asked.

"Hmmmmm?" Bill said slowly but clearly, "At 12:15 AM."

There was a pin-drop silence in the room after Bill announced the time.

"Brace yourselves, boys, there's a big match to face," Bill said as he was about to open the door to leave the room.

"Sir, surprise, no game strategy for this match?" asked Will, the goalkeeper, standing up.

"Boys, sometimes, survival is the best strategy," Bill replied and left the room.

Time: 10:15 PM

Bill ordered everyone not to leave the premises until he said so. In fact, he had asked security to lock the gates. Everyone was cursing Bill among themselves for ruining their Friday winter weekend fun.

Bill came into the boardroom. The Head Coach, Bob, stood up for instructions.

"Sir, I'm wondering, in fact kind of unhappy about this match on such short notice. And on the other hand, sorry to say, you're acting weird since afternoon. You're not revealing the whereabouts of the opposing team, not talking about anything. And what on earth, a match at midnight? Who are we playing against? Owls?" Bob sounded sarcastic.

Bill had immense respect for Bob, so he didn't get angry at his slightly rude words.

"Bob, I can't talk about it until it happens. Please trust me. It's for the best of all of you and for the future of our club only. Just make sure you drop the boys at the venue and come back from the entrance itself. DON'T STAY BACK."

"And everyone, please leave the office after the bus leaves the club."

Mark wanted to interrupt but, seeing Bill's serious face, he didn't dare to speak.

Time: 12:45 AM

Mark and Bob started running towards the club, broke open the gates, and ran towards the Director's room, using all their energy.

The door to Bill's room was closed. His car was outside, so he must be in the room. Both banged on the door, shouting for him. After five minutes, they broke open the door. Mark entered the room and started shouting, "Mark, there was a massacre there, why the hell aren't you picking up the call? We got the news from the neighborhood and there's a fire in the old stadium nearby, the place where you asked us to drop the boys. When we went there, we found the boys burned to ashes."

"Bill, everyone is dead, no one is left." Saying this, Mark collapsed, weeping uncontrollably.

Bob stepped into the room, searching for Bill. Bill was sitting on the sofa in the corner, on the opposite side. As they both approached the sofa, they were shocked to see Bill dead on the sofa! With a revolver in his right hand, he had shot himself in the temple. It seemed like he had died instantly. Shocked to the core, Bob and Mark found a letter in Bill's left hand.

Bob started reading the letter aloud.

"I am really sorry for whatever is going to happen, guys. But trust me, I never imagined this would happen to us. The letter is from The Pheonix Football Club, and we all know that no one can dare to reject their invitation. I can't spare our star teams in the hands of those ruthless people. I had to sacrifice someone. So I did, and the sacrifice ends with me."

Bob fainted upon reading the words "The Pheonix Football Club."

The next day, newspapers and electronic media reported the same news as Breaking News!

The horror legend had struck again!

Once upon a time, Soccer Legend, The Pheonix Football Club, was a pride for the states until Hitler invited the team to Stuttgart to play with their Nazianos FC. On December 4th, 1937, at 11:45 PM, under the floodlights, as the match started, Hitler came to watch the match. He was deeply humiliated by the shocking performance of his players and the utter dominance of the Pheonix team. He went crazy and ordered the soldiers to burn the Pheonix team to ashes, leaving no one alive.

That night, all 15 members of the team were burned to ashes, but there is a legend that their spirits rose from their ashes, sworn to burn every leading football team in the world. A curse on the whole world, who had merely witnessed their helpless death.

Every December 4th, a letter comes to the football team – it's not a letter, it's a curse!

Accept to Die or Die!

(The above work is pure fiction and is not part of any history. So let's not get into the digging part of it.)

THE GATE ACROSS THE ROAD – PART I

"And you said, her name is?", Dr. Oberoi inquired, his voice low yet focused. His piercing gaze, magnified by his glasses, was said to penetrate the depths of people's minds.

"Janaki Muthuraman, doctor," replied the man, dressed in traditional South Indian attire with a vermilion mark between his eyebrows.

Dr. Oberoi coughed, relaxing slightly in his chair as he glanced at the file in his hand. A pin-drop silence filled the room, broken only by the ticking of the wall clock.

The two visitors, a widowed woman in her early 50s and her son in his 30s, sat on the other side of the table, their eyes wide with anticipation.

Dr. Oberoi stood up, file in hand, and began pacing around the room. After a moment, he leaned against the wall, turned to the visitors, and asked respectfully, "Amma, you must be?"

The man replied, "She is my mother, doctor. Is there anything serious in the case, doctor?" His anxiety was evident.

"Well, Mr. Devaraja, this is a typical psychological disorder, affecting about 1 in 100 people. It's considerably stronger than the hallucinations Dr. Srinivasan noted in this case file," Dr. Oberoi explained.

"I'm sure if you had stayed in Khumbakonam, relied on local doctors, and waited for divine intervention, this case would have become more complicated, and we might not have been able to save her from this abnormal situation," he added.

He pressed the intercom, calling his secretary to bring coffee for three. "Dr. Bhagyarajan is my college mate and a family friend. I'll do my best to help her. Don't worry. We have the best doctors and psychiatrists who have handled hundreds of such cases. And most importantly, we have a state-of-the-art rehabilitation center that can cure her in no time," Dr. Oberoi assured them, sipping his coffee as he looked at them.

"Rehabilitation center?" the old lady asked, her eyes wide with surprise. She turned to her son, seeking clarification.

"Mental ward," he whispered in Tamil.

Her eyes widened, and she began to cry loudly, "Doctor, this would be a great disgrace to my family. My daughter-in-law in a mental hospital? We can't live normally in our society. People will pity us, and we can't bear that. God, why don't you just take her away?"

"Amma, relax! We'll take care of her. She's not going anywhere," her son comforted her, pulling her into his arms.

Dr. Oberoi cleared his throat and said, "Let's start the procedure tomorrow. Bring Janaki to our special wing at 8 AM. My secretary, Lisa, will guide you further."

The next day, Janaki, a beautiful and innocent housewife, entered the therapy room with her husband by her side. Her eyes were clouded with fear and confusion as she looked around at the unfamiliar surroundings.

A nurse approached her with a smile, gently took her hand away from her husband, and led her to a comfortable chair. She asked Janaki to relax while her husband waited in the lobby.

The nurse turned off the lights, creating a soothing atmosphere, and soft music began to play. As Janaki relaxed into the music, Dr. Oberoi emerged from behind a curtain and began to hypnotize her, guiding her into a deep sleep where she could respond to his questions.

"Janaki, before I start the countdown from 5 to 1, I will ask you simple questions," Dr. Oberoi said.

"What is your name, Janaki?" As he asked, he noticed a gentle smile on her lips.

"You just said my name, Janaki. Janaki Muthuraman," she replied in a low but clear voice.

"Where do you belong to?"

"I was born in a small village near Madurai, brought up in Madurai, and since my marriage, I have lived with my family in Khumbakonam."

"Education?"

"I have studied MA Literature on Tamil culture and heritage."

"Interests?"

"Not any as such, but before my marriage, I used to read a lot."

"Okay, Janaki! Relax and focus on my instructions. You are getting into a deep sleep as I start my countdown. 5, 4, 3, 2, 1..."

A deep silence fell over the room. Dr. Oberoi sat in a nearby chair for two minutes, then stood up and approached Janaki to give her further instructions. To his shock, she did not respond.

He took a deep breath and reached for her ears, saying, "You will be listening to me now, Janaki. This relaxation is good, let's make it better by answering my questions."

After a pause, Janaki began to murmur.

Dr. Oberoi approached her, "That's good, you are responding now. Now let's go back to your memories, shall we?"

"Otra mañana, otro día en mi vida, veo que, pero nunca llegó a por ello. Dios me ayude a llegar a ella, pronto, antes de que yo doy y morir..." she began to hum.

"Wakey, todo el mundo! el momento de pasar por el culo... los clientes comenzarán a llegar. obtener el café listo!"

Dr. Oberoi was utterly confused. His colleague, who was observing from the room, said through his Bluetooth earpiece, "She's speaking Spanish!"

"She said this: 'Another morning, another day in my life, I see that, but I never reached for it. God help me reach it, soon, before I give and die... Wakey wakey, everyone! time to move up your ass...customers will start coming. get the coffee ready!'"

Dr. Oberoi tried to recall the Spanish he had learned in college and approached Janaki, "Senora, ¡Buenos días!" (Lady, Good morning!)

Janaki replied, "Quién es este" (Who is this?)

Dr. Oberoi paused, trying to remember more Spanish words. His colleague prompted him through his earpiece to repeat the words he had said.

"Senora, Yo soy tu amigo" (Lady, I am your friend)

"Yo venía de una tierra lejana y estoy perdido" (I came from a distant land and I am lost)

"Puedes decirme dónde estamos" (Can you please tell me where are we)

Janaki began to laugh loudly with her eyes closed.

"¿Dónde estamos?" (Where are we?) she continued laughing.

"Estoy donde estoy... usted debe saber dónde se encuentra" (I am where I am... you should know where you are) she replied playfully.

Dr. Oberoi paused for a moment. This was definitely not Janaki, the introverted, soft-spoken, traditional South Indian housewife. The voice he heard was outgoing, dominating, and cheerful.

"Lo siento, lo suficiente como jugar con usted, usted está en las afueras de Buenos Aires" (Sorry, enough messing with you, you are just outside Buenos Aires)

"La hermosa, árbol de hoja perenne, seduciendo wilmaca condado" (The beautiful, evergreen, seducing wilmaca county)

Janaki began to sing a song.

"Dr. Oberoi, are you there?" his colleague shouted through his Bluetooth.

"Dr. Oberoi, this is a simple case. Janaki must have been influenced by Spanish culture or Latin countries through friends or visits. This can be easily solved."

"Dr. Mehta, Janaki has never stepped out of Tamil Nadu in her entire life. She barely knows English. Let alone Spanish friends, she has no friends at all. How on earth is this possible?"

For the first time, Dr. Oberoi faced his toughest case. He was clueless about where to start. Just as he was getting lost in his thoughts, he remembered that he needed to wake Janaki up.

As he approached Janaki to give her the wake-up instructions, she pushed him aside, sat up straight, and exclaimed, "¡Qué es esto sin sentido, qué estás tratando de hacer!" (What is this nonsense, what are you trying to do?)

"Usted entró en mi café como un caballero y ahora usted ha traído mí en algún lugar desconocido. Yo debería haber escuchado a mi padre borracho, nunca hablo con foriegners. Voy a patearte, si usted no me dejó salir y volver a mi casa." (You stepped into my cafe like a gentleman and now you have brought me somewhere unknown. I should have listened to my drunken father, Never talk to foreigners. I will kick you, if you don't let me out and back to my place.)

As Janaki said this, she pushed Dr. Oberoi into the corner, causing him to hit his head against the wall and slowly slide down to his knees.

"Is that a ghost... a paranormal activity... bad spirits that have captured Janaki?"

Dr. Oberoi was filled with doubt as he fainted on the floor.

THE GATE ACROSS THE ROAD – PART II

"What just happened?" Dr. Oberoi asked, the first words out of his mouth as he regained consciousness.

He was lying on a bed, surrounded by his worried colleagues and secretary. With difficulty, he sat up, his secretary supporting his neck. A sharp pain throbbed in his head.

Dr. Oberoi paced the hall, lost in thought. He felt foolish for his earlier speculations about spirits, ghosts, or black magic.

"I'm glad I didn't say that out loud," he muttered to himself.

Within an hour, he made a decision. Janaki was admitted as an in-house patient at the rehabilitation center. Her husband and mother-in-law signed the necessary paperwork after a brief disagreement. The nurses escorted Janaki to a secure room, barring visitors.

Strong doses of medication were administered to keep Janaki unconscious.

Dr. Oberoi contacted his college friend, Dr. Steeve, a renowned neuroscientist and expert in critical psychological disorders. Steeve, fluent in eight languages, agreed to come to Mumbai that weekend.

Relieved, Dr. Oberoi instructed his secretary to book tickets and accommodations for Steeve.

The next day, as Dr. Oberoi arrived at his office, his anxious secretary had news to share. "Doctor, we didn't mean to interrupt your guest lecture, but Janaki woke up early this morning. The nurse on duty said she opened her eyes, spoke in Tamil, asked for her family, and begged to be released. Then, she started cursing everyone in Spanish, and the nurse had to give her a dose to calm her down."

Dr. Oberoi was momentarily furious that he had not been informed about Janaki's condition. He managed to control his anger and said, "Steeve will be here tomorrow. Continue the dosage and ensure her proper nutrition. Most importantly, I need a Spanish translator here within the next hour. They should sit with her and record everything she says in English."

Dr. Oberoi spent the entire day focused on Janaki's past, setting aside all other cases. Janaki was born into a middle-class Brahmin family in southern Tamil Nadu on an inauspicious day of the Hindu calendar. Her birth was considered unlucky, and no one visited her newborn baby. To add to the tragedy, her mother died the next day from internal bleeding.

The family, including her father, labeled Janaki a demon, believing she had brought misfortune upon them. They abandoned her on the outskirts of the village. Fortunately, her grandmother rescued her and cared for her until she was ten. During those ten years, no one in the village spoke to or acknowledged Janaki.

Her grandmother eventually decided to send Janaki to a Christian missionary school, hoping she would receive better care and education.

"Religion won't save you, Janaki. But belief will!" were her grandmother's final words.

The missionary school marked a new beginning for Janaki. Surrounded by orphans like herself, she experienced friendship for the first time. However, the deep wounds of her childhood prevented her from fully opening up. She found solace in Marie, her only friend, who remained by her side until Janaki's marriage.

Dr. Oberoi searched for Marie's current contact information and discovered she was working with the Red Cross in Cochin. Through his network, he managed to get her number.

He learned that Marie was currently busy at a workshop but would be available at six.

"Six, huh?" Dr. Oberoi muttered to himself, realizing he hadn't eaten lunch. He called his secretary to order something from Subway.

Before he could finish speaking, his secretary interrupted loudly, "Doctor, listen! Me and the translator are coming to your room. You need to hear this."

A few minutes later, they joined Dr. Oberoi in his room. There was a brief silence before the translator began speaking.

"Throughout the day, Janaki has been talking about various things, like needing to hire more people for her café. She's concerned about money and wants to save more. She's even decided not to buy a new dress or throw a party for her friends. She's so close to achieving her dream," the translator said.

"But every 15 minutes, she sings a Spanish poem. She's sung it about 100 times so far," she added.

Dr. Oberoi became more focused and took the papers from the translator, starting to read the transcript. For the next hour, there was complete silence as he immersed himself in the words.

Just as the clock struck six, the phone rang. Dr. Oberoi answered without hesitation, "Hi Marie, I'm waiting for you. This is Dr. Oberoi from Mumbai. Your friend Janaki is undergoing treatment for her abnormal psychic behavior here. We need your help understanding the pattern."

There was a pause on the line. After a minute, Marie's voice trembled as she replied, "Is Janu fine?"

"She's physically fine, but she's trapped in a psychological dilemma. In recent months, she's been speaking strangely when she wakes up. She'll seem normal for a while, but then she'll start cursing everyone in Spanish, a language none of her family understands. Lately, she's stopped speaking as Janaki, the South Indian woman. Instead, she calls herself Amelie and claims to be from Argentina."

"Amelie?" Marie repeated, seeking clarification.

"Does that name mean anything to you? Was she a friend from the hostel?" Dr. Oberoi asked eagerly.

"No, Doctor," Marie replied. "Amelie is the name of the girl in the poem we used to recite in school."

"A group of gospel singers from Spain visited our hostel and taught us the song. It's called 'The Gate Across the Road,'" she explained.

Dr. Oberoi quickly reviewed the transcript and began reading the translated poem:

There is a gate across the road Beyond the gate,

lies the world's beautiful garden Garden full of trees.

Beyond the trees lies the biggest grape yard.

In the grape yard, lies the dark grapes Whose taste is much talked about in the city of Buenos Aires and around.

There lived a beautiful girl called Amelie who lives in a hut opposite the gate.

Daughter of a drunkard…Amelie always sits on the pavement and hums the most beautiful songs.

he always dreams to step into the garden beyond the gates.

But is scared of her father, scared of the monster gate keeper.

She waited for days, weeks and months to get into the garden One fine day she crossed the road,

when her father was asleep Mindful of fantasies, she carried all the way about how she gonna

Enjoy the sweetness of the fruits, smell the fragrance of flowers Play in the lush greens with rabbits….

Just as her mind full of joysome dreams, eyes full of excitement reach the peaks,

Held her by claws…took her to somewhere, far and distant….

As she flew to the sky, she caught the glimpse of the vast grape yards and apple trees inside..

But alas she couldn't taste it…..

May be in next life, she thought, as the eagle claws tightened around her neck…

Marie said, "Yes, it sounds the same. But the Spanish poem is so beautiful. Of all 24 girls from our hostel, Janaki is the only one who could memorize the whole song and sing it all the time."

"Initially, I thought Janaki was just in love with the song," Marie continued. "But after a year or so, she told me she didn't like Amelie dying in the poem. She related herself to Amelie, saying she could have died if her parents hadn't abandoned her. Luckily, she had her grandmother. But she always said Amelie had no one to rescue her."

"For years, aside from her studies, Janaki empathized with Amelie. She imagined Amelie being rescued from the eagle's claws and cared for by God in a safe land," Marie explained.

She took a deep breath and continued, "I always thought Janaki would eventually grow out of her obsession with Amelie. But to my surprise, the night before her marriage, she told me, 'I'm happy I'm getting married, but Amelie is still single. Many men are interested in her. She's become the most beautiful woman in town.'"

"I scolded Janaki and told her to stop this nonsense," Marie said. "Her new family wouldn't understand. Janaki came closer and said, 'I can't do that, because I am Amelie now. She grew up with me every minute and every second. I can't leave her. Every night I close my eyes, Amelie starts her day. I make sure Amelie gets plenty of time to fulfill her dreams. That's why I sleep late in the morning.'"

"Amelie has grown up independently now," Marie said. "She owns a coffee shop, teaches music to children, and is even planning to buy the garden. She says there won't be any gates to restrict children from entering and enjoying the beauty."

Marie paused, then added, "I listened to everything she shared and took a promise from her that she will not discuss any of this it with her new family."

Dr. Oberoi thanked Marie for sharing Janaki's past and hung up the phone.

"Let's wait for Steeve to arrive tomorrow," he said to his secretary and the translator. He grabbed his coat and keys, ready to leave for home. Just before stepping out the door, he instructed, "Call her family tomorrow. Ask them to be here by nine."

The next day, Steeve and Dr. Oberoi met in the hallway outside Janaki's room. They discussed the case over coffee, and Steeve concluded that the situation was serious.

"To make Janaki normal, we need to eliminate Amelie," Steeve said. "In other words, we need to 'kill' her off. But there's always a risk to Janaki's life."

"Let's not waste time here," Dr. Oberoi agreed. "We need to take her to my lab, but first, we need her family's consent."

Dr. Oberoi called Janaki's husband and mother-in-law to meet with Steeve. As they approached, Steeve introduced himself.

"Will she be okay?" Janaki's husband asked, his voice filled with despair.

"Why don't you just euthanize her, doctor?" Janaki's mother-in-law said harshly. "She's a disgrace to our family. I told my son that day he was crazy for wanting to marry her." She began to cry.

Dr. Oberoi interrupted her. "Look, amma, she's just like you, a human being, but with a small problem. Please be patient, and I appreciate it if you could refrain from using such harsh language. After the troubled childhood she endured, she deserves support and cooperation from all of us."

Steeve opened the door to Janaki's room, and everyone followed. Janaki was awake, staring at the ceiling, calm and unresisting.

Steeve instructed the nurse to untie her, but Dr. Oberoi cautioned him. Steeve insisted.

Janaki stood up and began walking, wincing at the marks on her wrists from being tied to the bed. Her wrists were swollen and red, and blood was oozing from one of them. Yet, her eyes remained calm and free of pain.

Everyone in the room watched her anxiously, especially her mother-in-law, who clung tightly to her son's arm, hiding behind him in fear.

Steeve spoke to Janaki. "How are you doing?"

She stopped and turned, replying in Spanish, " Usted gente grosera, están perjudicando a Janaki mucho. Ella no se merece esto. Para el tipo de favor que me hizo, me hace vivir, que le está dando un gran castigo" (You rude people are hurting Janaki a lot. She doesn't deserve this. For the kind of favor she did for me, allowing me to live, you're punishing her severely.")

"Amelie, aunque no queremos eso. Usted es el mejor uno para darnos la solución. Dejar de hacer Janaki de no sufrir. Déjala y van …("Amelie," Steeve replied in a gentle yet firm voice, "even we don't want that. You're the best one to give us the solution. Stop making Janaki suffer. Leave her and go...")

Janaki laughed uncontrollably for the next two minutes, as everyone continued to stare at her in utter confusion.

"Te crees que soy un fantasma que la dejo …… dejar de bromear … Yo soy de la idea, soy la creencia … Janaki tiene en su mente. Tan fuerte que no se puede hacer nada con los tratamientos disponibles en el mundo. ("Do you think I'm a ghost that can just leave her? Stop joking around. I am the idea, the belief... lodged so deeply in Janaki's mind that no treatments currently available can help)", said Janaki, sitting in the nearby chair.

"Tengo la solución para ello. Pero usted tiene que creer en mí a ciegas. Entonces sólo yo puedo ayudarte.

La confianza es la palabra. Están preparados para ello? " (I have the solution for it," Janaki said, looking into Steeve's eyes. "But you have to believe in me completely. Only then can I help you. Trust is the key. Are you all ready for that?")

Steeve too looked into her eyes with utmost focus, trying to read her mind.

After a few minutes, he called everyone closer and prepared them to follow her instructions.

"Steeve, this is incredibly risky," Dr. Oberoi said, unconvinced. "You're putting all your faith in her."

"We have to do this, Dr. Oberoi," Steeve replied firmly. "It's our only option."

"Estamos preparados? (Are we ready?)", Janaki shouted.

"Sí, lo estamos, señora. No te voy a molestar más. Somos todo tuyo. Voy a traducir lo que cada vez que usted está diciendo para el entendimiento ("Yes, we are, lady," Steeve responded. "I won't interrupt you anymore. We are all yours. I will translate everything you say for everyone's understanding.")

"Aceptar. todos vienen cerca y ponte sobre tus rodillas. cierra los ojos y mantenga su mano derecha en mi mano. ("Okay," Janaki agreed. "Come closer, everyone, and kneel down. Close your eyes and hold my right hand in yours." She reached out to them.)

Steeve started translating for everyone. Within a minute, everyone followed the instructions.

They all held their hands in Janaki's hand. Janaki closed their hands together with her other hand and began to speak, "Gracias por confiar en mí. Mi vida está en deuda con Janaki por hacerme vivir mi sueño en el sueño. Gracias a Janaki, su vida se convierten en mi vida. Una vida que había estado esperando durante años para obtener de forma. Libertad para mi padre borracho, la ausencia de control de la sociedad. Una vida de mis propios términos. Un dueño de mi propio destino. Todo eso sucedió debido a Janaki. Cada noche Janaki cerró los ojos, para asegurarse de que deambulo en mi jardín favorito, jugar en mis calles favoritas.

La puerta no es mi puerta de entrada a la libertad. Camina conmigo y me siga a mi mundo. No te pregunta a ti mismo. Dont dudo. Sólo sígueme, porque yo soy nunca a hacer daño o manipular ("Thanks for trusting me. My life is forever indebted to Janaki for allowing me to live my dream within her own. Because of Janaki, her life became mine – a life I yearned for for years. Freedom from my drunken father, freedom from societal control. A life on my own terms, a master of my own destiny. All thanks to Janaki. Every night Janaki closed her eyes, to make sure that I wandered in my favorite garden and played in my favorite streets.

The door there is my gateway to freedom. Walk with me and follow me to my world. Don't question yourself. Don't doubt it. Just follow me, because I am never to harm you or manipulate you.")

Janaki slowly stood up, and everyone else followed suit. Everyone's eyes were closed, and they were in a trance.

Without taking her hands off theirs, she slowly moved towards the door, and everyone followed her. As she reached the door, she said, "Al abrir la puerta y mudo, yo concedo a mí mismo la libertad de estos embragues. No te abre los ojos, hasta que yo lo diga y no te dejar mis manos, hasta que yo lo diga. (As I open the door and move out, I am granting myself freedom from these clutches. Don't open your eyes until I say so, and don't let go of my hands until I say so.)

She released their hands and slowly opened the door, walking towards the other side. Everyone followed her.

As they entered the other side, a cool breeze enveloped them, and a bright light shone into their eyes, but no one opened their eyes.

Ahora, sin abrir los ojos, sólo lentamente despegar las manos y quitarse los zapatos y esperar a que mis instrucciones adicionales. (Now, without opening your eyes, just slowly take off your hands and shoes, and wait for my further instructions.)

Everyone followed her instructions. As they removed their shoes and sandals and felt the ground, they experienced a pleasant sensation under their feet.

A strange yet pleasant feeling washed over everyone's minds, but no one reacted to it.

"Now open up and don't get excited or nervous about what you see, "Ahora abra y no te emociones o gire nervioso a lo que se ve", she shouted in an energetic tone.

Everyone opened their eyes, and their disbelief was palpable. The door had opened not to the hospital corridor, but to a beautiful, brightly colored garden with a vineyard in the distance.

"We've never been here before," Dr. Oberoi murmured.

Steeve, too, was in a trance, but he tried to make sense of the situation. "We are in the garden where Amelie loved to be," he said.

In front of them stood Janaki, transformed into a beautiful Latina woman wearing a long skirt and humming a song.

Gracias por dejar que me fuera, aquí voy a mi árbol. Música, naturaleza, café, todo me está esperando. (Thanks for letting me out. Here I go to my tree. Music, nature, coffee – everything is waiting for me." With that, she turned back and walked towards the tree)

Janaki, lo siento, Amelie, ayúdanos a volver .... por favor .... (Janaki, sorry, Amelie, Steeve pleaded in a deep voice. "Help us go back... please..." He, along with everyone else – Dr. Oberoi, Janaki's husband, and mother-in-law – were utterly shocked and helpless.)

"Dont muchachos te preocupes, no te voy a encadenar aquí. Sólo cierra los ojos y dar la vuelta. El truco es Dont belive esto sucedió realmente. Todo va a estar normal. Abra la puerta y volver. Su Janaki está esperando allí .... Adiós" ("Don't worry, fellas. I won't chain you here. Just close your eyes and turn back. The trick is to not believe this actually happened. Everything will be normal. Open the door and go back. Your Janaki is waiting for you there... goodbye!)

With that, the Spanish girl, Amelie, vanished into the grape yard without looking back.

MY F*****R

"I've never been an outcast, not even in my dreams. I'm a loner at heart. Life has taught me the hardest lessons, leaving me alone to deal with all the crap that comes my way. God has been so kind to me and my sister, teaching us the philosophy of life by taking our parents away at a young age. My sister was struggling to understand the difference between day and night when she was still a child."

My memories flooded back to my childhood – temples, festivals, narrow streets, friendly neighbors, a doting mother, and a reclusive father! The image of my father in my mind interrupted my brief nap and pulled me back to reality as I opened my eyes and looked around. The train had arrived at Stockholm station. Early February in Stockholm didn't mean anything to Mr. Winter. He had a ruthless spell over the people, as I could see them bundled up in thick coats and caps everywhere.

As I walked through the streets, passing the famous Stockholm City Hall with a map in hand, memories flooded my mind. I was effortlessly finding my way without asking anyone. It was strange! Sweden is a beautiful country – vast lands, meadows surrounding the cities, stunning architecture, and delicious food – but with fewer people. I couldn't help but compare it to India.

I still remember our family tailor, Ashfaaq miya. He had 18 children, all living in a tiny 10x10-foot room with some space outside. We jokingly referred to him as the Prime Minister of Mini India. Those were lovely days!

The narrow lane beside the city hall led me to a wide circle with numerous florist shops. The air was filled with a fresh fragrance. I stopped for a moment to enjoy the moment.

"You don't need to get me jewels to make me happy," my mom used to say to my father. "Once in a while, some nice flowers make me happy." As his image came into my mind, a sudden shock jolted me awake.

Pandit Murali Sharma – that name alone tops my hate list. He was the person who left my family in ruins and abandoned us in the worst imaginable situation.

I still remember that day. My mom pawned her ring to buy groceries for my hungry sister and me. For the last five years, she struggled to make ends meet while my reclusive, lost father sat near the tree outside our house, disconnected from our family. I couldn't recall a single good moment with my father.

My mother was shocked to the core. She collapsed into the fire and was burned alive. Neither my young uncle nor I could save her from that fate. She died instantly, reduced to ashes.

Tears welled up in my eyes, but I didn't cry that day. If I cried, my little sister would too. I didn't attend the funeral or participate in the rituals. I simply said, 'I don't know him.'

I sat on a bench, taking deep breaths to ground myself. 'Why am I getting lost like this?' I asked myself. 'I've been so focused on life. Come back, be normal.' I reassured myself."

"As I looked across the road, I saw it – the place I'd come for. In that moment, it felt like it had found me. I crossed the road and entered the hall. The board outside read: AUCTION OPEN.

A life-size poster of Steve, with the tagline 'The man who rocked the world,' was at the bottom. Steve Crooney, aka Steve or Claws, was the lead singer of Holy Venom, the most famous rock band of the 80s and 90s. I grew up with their music, thanks to the missionary community where I lived. Brother Charles, my senior, often said, 'Music is a way to reach God. Love it, enjoy it, and you'll find Him. Master it, and you'll become Him.'

During my darkest times, Steve's voice and lyrics were a guardian that helped me find my way back to life. I always credit one of his songs, 'I Don't Want to See What Is Tomorrow,' with changing my life."

From an orphanage boy, I grew up slowly but steadily, took care of my sister, and with my decent pedigree in industrial engineering, landed a job in Frankfurt, Germany. When I got the offer, I was overjoyed because it would give me a chance to meet my lifelong idol, Steve, who lived just a night away from Frankfurt.

But to my utter disappointment, Steve had passed away 15 days earlier from a heart attack at 62 in his home in Stockholm. I couldn't attend the funeral due to tight deadlines for a product release at my company.

However, I could make it today for a final visit to his world, his belongings, his music notes, and to meet his band members – Mighty Joe, the drummer, and others.

As I walked into the gallery, amidst a crowd of admirers who had come to buy some of his auctioned items, I saw a few Bollywood celebrities who had also come to take a piece of Steve back to India. I walked through the line, admiring his legendary outfits he had worn for the Emmys and Billboard Rock Festival. He was truly the 'god who rocked the world,' I thought to myself.

As I was about to turn right into the second hall of his instruments, I saw a note on a high stand. It was the only item on display behind glass with a sign that read: 'DON'T TOUCH IT. NOT FOR AUCTION. ONLY FOR DISPLAY.'

I moved closer to the glass to examine the book carefully. The book had a Swastika mark with turmeric on the front cover and on the back cover was written: 'Aslam Publishers Ismai Ganj Varanasi.'

Varanasi, my hometown, how could Steve have obtained a book from Varanasi, India? And how could it be a normal notebook we kids used to write our homework in, like the music notes?

I was shocked and surprised, standing there for minutes, until a tall, well-built old man, Big Joe, came to me and placed a hand on my shoulder.

'Mister, it seems you and your time have frozen at this spot. There's a lot to check out about Steve. Why don't you step into that room too?'

'Mr. Joe, I'm from Varanasi. The book in that glass frame might have some answers for some questions. Can you please tell me about it?'

Joe looked straight into my eyes for a few seconds, took a deep breath with his hands on his hips, and said, 'Come with me, Kiddo.' He carefully removed the book from the frame, walked onto the balcony, and sat in a chair.

I followed the book and the hands that held it onto the balcony, sitting in the chair opposite him, waiting for him to open up.

Steve and I had kept this secret for a long time, but he revealed it to the rest of the band and his family on his deathbed. The reason for Steve and Holy Venom's enduring success in the music world is entirely attributed to the amazing and inspiring lyrics from this book. The lyrics were not written by Steve, and the book did not belong to him.

In the late 90s, when Holy Venom suffered a devastating blow with the sudden death of their lead singer, Kim, who had a drug overdose, Steve, Kim's best friend, came to India to scatter Kim's ashes in the Ganges, as per Kim's request. Steve and I arrived in Varanasi on a Friday, went to the Ganges, performed the rituals, and were walking back to the market to do some shopping.

I couldn't help but notice a middle-aged man following us for the last two hours since we had arrived. He followed us to the market and was at a distance, watching us and trying to find an opportunity to talk to us

I suddenly turned back, grabbed him by the collar, looked into his eyes, and fiercely said, "Either you stop following us, or I'll kick your ass and drag you to the police!" Then I shoved him so hard that the thin man flew about 10 feet away.

Steve watched the whole thing, his face completely expressionless, looking puzzled.

Slowly, the man got up, walked over to Steve, and started speaking in the gentlest tone, in English: "Look, Steve, I'm not here to harm you or steal from you. I don't have time for that. I have something important to show you."

Saying this, he took out some notes from his satchel and handed them to Steve.

Steve flipped through the pages of the notebook and stopped at one. He read it for a few minutes, then closed his eyes. When he opened them, I could see an amazing spark in his gaze.

He grabbed the man by the shoulders with overwhelming enthusiasm and asked, "Who are you, man? A musical genius? Why are you here? These are the most incredible lyrics I've ever seen in my life! I'm telling you, this will make you famous overnight, turn you into an icon. Here's the deal—come with us to London. Be part of our band, work with us, please!"

Arrogant and aggressive by nature, Steve—the rising star of the rock world—found himself on his knees for the first time in his life before a seemingly ordinary man from the slums of India.

The man showed no emotion. In a calm voice, he said, "I have 100 lyrics and the music notes for them. I don't have time. Just buy them from me. I need the money, that's all."

"I'm ready to pay you, how much do you want?" Steve asked.

"Fifty thousand," the man replied. "Cash."

"Look, man, I'm willing to pay you more than that. But I only have fifteen thousand on me right now. You'll have to come with me to the hotel. I can cash in some traveler's cheques and give you the rest."

The man interrupted Steve, raising his voice impatiently. "Give me whatever you have. That's enough for me."

He took the money, pocketed it without even counting, and walked away without looking back.

As he left, I heard him say, "No matter what, don't lose that book. Take care of it."

Steve did exactly that. From that moment on, there was no stopping Steve and Holy Venom. A year later, our comeback concert in Vienna became the defining moment of our careers.

Steve's voice, combined with the band's magical music, brought those lyrics to life. The world has been listening to and loving all 100 songs, with only minor modifications here and there.

"I Don't Want to See What's Tomorrow"—that track was the most powerful of all. It was closest to the man's heart (as he mentioned in the book) and to Steve's as well. And you know how much the fans adored it.

Steve traveled to India many times after that, searching for that man, but he never found him. We both kept this secret, revealing it to our families and the band only recently, just before Steve passed away.

In his final moments, Steve said to me, "My life, up until this very minute, is because of that man. I owe everything to him."

The poor man had left a note for his family, especially for his son, on the last page of the book—a note I remember Steve reading many times.

Mighty Joe then turned to the final page and read it aloud to me:

"Son, by the time you read this, I may no longer be in this world. I can only imagine the hatred you must feel toward me—for leaving you, your mom, and your sister in such a helpless situation. But you need to understand, my life has been filled with helplessness, too. A life where you have dreams, aspirations, and, most importantly, the talent to achieve them, but the harsh limitations of reality hold you back, leaving you feeling crippled.

A middle-class Brahmin, born into a conservative and orthodox family in a remote village in India, doesn't dare to dream of becoming a rock star. I suppressed my passion for my parents, then for my family. But how long could I remain silent? At some point, living a life without pursuing your dreams, living a life with no meaning, becomes worse than not living at all.

But despite everything, I love you. You must know that. I will always take care of you and the family, wherever I am."

As Mighty Joe read those words, I nearly fell to my knees, feeling a deep, unshakable connection to someone or something close. Then Joe said the name: Pandit Murali Sharma.

I sat down on the floor, closing my eyes, as memories flashed before me like a reel of film. All the moments of my life suddenly made sense. The mysterious scholarship I received in high school—I could now feel it was my father's doing, the father I had spent my whole life hating.

With tears in my eyes, I looked at Mighty Joe and whispered, "He's my father. Thank you for bringing me back to him.

THE CYCLE

The wall, damp and covered in fungus and green moss, feels like a beautiful park to me. Crawling on it is like your stroll through Wonderland—at least from what I've gathered about the human world and its dreams. The cloudy sky, with rain looming, creates the perfect atmosphere for a leisurely crawl and to plan my early dinner.

My transformation is coming soon, and this life of crawling will soon be behind me. The world's current disdain for my ugly appearance will soon turn to admiration. Children will sing nursery rhymes about me, men will compare their lovers to me, and women will long to adorn themselves in colors like mine. Oh yes, I will soon be the darling of the world!

Lost in my dreams of a colorful future, I suddenly lost control as a gust of wind from the east caught me off guard. Boom! I was about to crash to the floor, bidding farewell to my dreams—and my life—but I landed on something soft. Thank goodness, I'm safe!

Regaining my balance, I crawled a few inches on the surface to see where I'd landed. It was a human body. I crept over his chest and looked up at his face—an old man, perhaps in his eighties. His frail muscles had no strength left to brush me off, and his body showed no instinct to recoil. Normally, when I accidentally fall on a human, they scream, shout, and flail as if the world is ending and they'll be the first to perish. But this man was different, or perhaps it was just his weakness. Lucky me.

Slowly, I crawled up his neck, past his mouth, and finally settled on his nose, peering into his pale eyes. He noticed me, but there was no panic, no urgency in his gaze. He simply stared at me.

Minutes passed, and we continued to look into each other's eyes. Then, tears rolled down his cheeks. I could sense the deep sorrow within him. His eyes told me everything. Humans may have a thousand ways to communicate, but the language of the eyes is universal—understood by every creature, including me.

"You're the first living thing to touch me in the last 15 days," he began softly. "Everyone has left me here to die. My illness, which is contagious, has driven them all away. Even the nurse who used to visit every week has stopped coming. My food comes through tubes now, fed through the window. But for the last three days, even that has stopped. They must be waiting for me to die—hoping for it."

I let him speak, letting him pour out his sorrow, lightening his heart just a little.

"I deserve this, maybe," he continued. "I came into this world pure, but I learned selfishness and manipulation from those around me. I passed those same lessons on to my children. And now, they're returning the favor, giving me back the same coldness I once showed others."

I listened silently, my tiny heart struggling to carry the weight of his grief. I wanted to say, "I can't handle this much sadness—I'm about to get my transformation soon. I need to prepare for that."

His eyes brightened for a moment. "Oh, you're about to change? That's wonderful. I'm so happy for you. Isn't it strange how you start as something ugly and transform into something beautiful, while we humans come into the world as something beautiful and end up rotting away? Some say the lucky ones, when they die, take on a beautiful form like yours. I'm waiting for that."

I felt a glimmer of hope. "So you'll join me soon? Promise we'll continue our conversations."

A question lingered in his eyes. "But how will you recognize me?"

I crawled off his nose and back onto the wall. Turning back to him after a few moments, I said, "We both need friends for the journey we're about to begin."

A few days passed.

In common terms, I "died" and was reborn, but in the world's most beautiful and colorful form. Nature had blessed me with her brightest colors, and as I woke, fluttering my wings, there was a gentle, pleasant feeling all around. I was happy—but there was still an emptiness. I needed to find him.

I flew to the room where he had lived, but it was empty. His bed was gone, and outside, people were talking in hushed tones. From the atmosphere, I knew he had passed. I was happy for him. I couldn't wait to see him again.

I followed the trail to the burial ground and found his grave, freshly dug with a stone that read "Rest in Peace."

"Rest in peace?" I thought. "You left him to rot while he was alive, and now you say rest in peace? What a joke."

I waited patiently on a nearby tree, watching the grave. After hours of waiting, as the last person left, I saw it—a beautiful butterfly emerging from the earth, its wings fluttering toward the sky.

My joy was boundless. I flew to meet him, and when he turned to face me, he smiled. "Look at you, the ugly caterpillar, so beautiful now."

"Compliments later," I teased. "Let's see who can fly higher!"

Together, our colorful wings beat faster as we soared into the blue sky, leaving trails of vibrant colors behind us.

THE STORY OF XX & XY

X was waiting on a dark street, where streams of water rushed by with an unprecedented force. Just across the road stood a replica of X, waiting in the same anxious and nervous stance. Two alien figures began to appear, their forms becoming clearer as they approached. As they neared, it became evident that these figures were also X and Y. Y approached the X on this side of the street, while X and Y crossed to meet the other X on the opposite side. Without asking for permission, Y confidently hugged X and kissed her. "Come, it's time to get ready for the journey. We need to get into our berth soon," Y said.

As XY hurried towards the magical berth waiting for them at the end of the street, the other pair, XX, stopped them.

XY looked at them carelessly. "I'm meant to go out soon, so you'd better make way for me."

XX replied confidently, "I have as much of a chance to go out as you do."

Laughing loudly, XY threw a dismissive glance at XX. "I am destined to rule the world. I am meant to invent, create, and enjoy. Don't worry, you'll have your chance too—if not now, then maybe in the next lifetime!" XY burst out laughing.

"I am as much as you, aspiring to live in the world out there. God gave us equal rights," XX responded. "Let's stop this argument, because it will become a daily routine with your kind once I'm out. How about we settle this with a race to the berth? The first one to touch it gets to go."

XY was silent for a moment, taking a deep breath before glancing sideways at XX. "Let's do it, if you have the nerve to watch yourself lose," XY said, before forcefully pushing XX to the ground and sprinting toward the magical berth, which had begun glowing more brightly as it watched the pair race down the street.

XY ran victoriously, dreams of the outside world flooding his mind, imagining how special he would feel when he arrived. But suddenly, a flash of lightning shot past XY and, in an instant, touched the destination. There, sitting on the stairs and gasping for breath, was XX.

XY was astonished. Despite being pushed to the ground, XX had reached the finish with ease. Stunned, XY slowed his run and walked toward her.

"You ran to defeat me. I ran to make myself win. That's the difference," XX said, standing up. Slowly, the magical berth opened, giving XX a place to step inside.

"You have no idea what a foolish act you're about to commit!" XY shouted. "Don't you understand? You're not meant to be born—I am. In fact, everyone in the family prayed for me, not you. If you're born, they'll consider you a curse. I am meant to bring them luck. Do you really want to be the one cursed by your family?"

XX paused and turned to face XY, who continued, "Do you know her in-laws consulted 100 priests to decide on the most auspicious time for my birth? The union of him and her was not about love, but prestige and the ego of the family. They're all anxiously awaiting me, not you."

XX remained silent, lost in thought, as XY tried to manipulate her. "You have no chance like I do to live and enjoy the world. First of all, if you are born, you'll have slim chances of surviving. The family waiting for me will kill you and throw you into the drain in no time. Even if you survive, your life will be hell. You'll face torture, abuse, and rape. Is that what you want?"

XY's voice grew more confident, expecting to see XX defeated by his words. But XX cleared her throat, stood up straight, and took a deep breath.

"Thank you for your kind and 'realistic' words," she replied. "But despite all these obstacles, don't you think I too can have the determination and will to live? Maybe I'll stand and fight."

"You can't," XY shouted authoritatively. "You're weak, and you'll be filled with fear."

"I have hope, and I'm clear," XX shouted back. She stepped into the berth and closed the door behind her, waiting for her time to come. All the fears created by XY vanished, replaced by a dream of her being greeted and welcomed by the world when she stepped out.

All this took place in the belly of a helpless pregnant mother in a remote village of India, on an ordinary day, where female feticide had become as common as drinking water.

AND SO WE MOVE ON WITH LOVE…………..

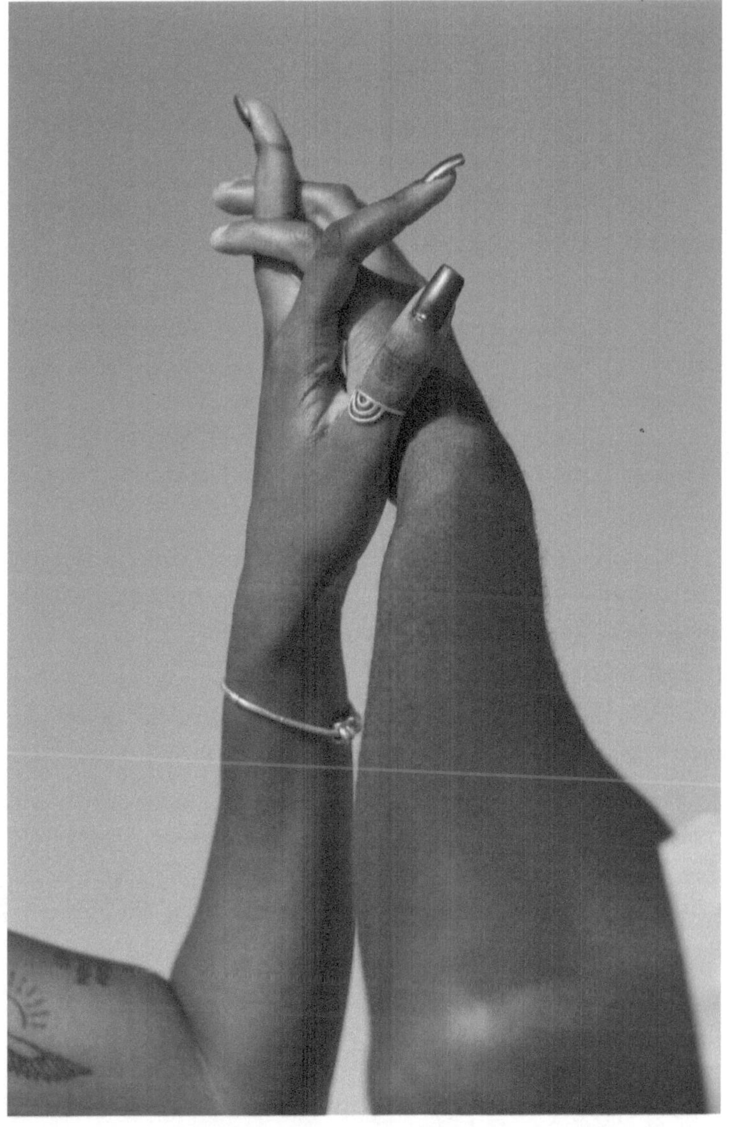

"I'm sorry," slipped from Adi's lips, a whisper lost in the heavy silence.

Nidhi, her head resting on the table, was crying silently. She pulled away, her face turned away from him, her voice filled with a raw, unspoken pain, "Sorry? Is that all you can say now, Adi? S-O-R-R-Y... it spells like that, I guess. Or do you even know the meaning of it, you heartless jerk?"

Her anger was a tempest, threatening to consume her. She wanted to lash out, to hurt him, but couldn't.

"Nidhi, I genuinely mean it. I'm deeply sorry for everything that's happened. I can't undo the past or bring back the good times, but I truly feel like I hurt you badly with my silence."

"Ha ha ha... bring back our times? What a joke! Adi, you always talk about things you can't do. You never made an effort to fix things when it mattered. I've known you inside and out since the day I met you in the library. What a fool I was to fall for your good looks, sweet words, surprise gifts, candlelit dinners, long drives, and daydreams. I've imagined us in every fantasy you've created, but I never saw the real you."

"But when the dreams fade, castles crumble, and candles melt, reality hits hard. It hit me every second, in the form of you, making me regret my decision," Nidhi collapsed against the wall, weeping, her sobs echoing through the room.

Adi stood in the center of the room, his face devoid of expression, but a single tear rolled down his cheek as he watched Nidhi's pain.

Outside the room, in the hall, several people were sitting on sofas and mats, whispering among themselves. Older women were crying loudly, their sobs a mournful chorus. An elderly man was trying to console the most devastated woman in the room, his words offering little comfort.

Adi turned his head to Nidhi, his voice a hoarse whisper, "Nidhi, do you think that in our seven years together, all I did was manipulate you? All I created was a false mirage that you chased? Do you think my heart has no space for you, or that I don't love you? Please answer me," he asked, his eyes filled with a desperate plea.

Nidhi bluntly said, "Yes, you're a liar and a cheat who ruined my life."

Tears started streaming down Adi's face uncontrollably as he tried to sit down, overcome by her harsh words. His voice, filled with sorrow, barely audible, "Nidhi, these words have broken me completely. Even God won't forgive me when I meet him. But I need to tell you one truth, the last one before we part forever."

"Nidhi, I was madly and deeply in love with you from the moment I met you until this very moment, even when your words tore me apart. The only difference is that before marriage, I had dreams for us, and after marriage, I worked to make them a reality, one by one, big and small. Believe it or not, every thought I invested during these years was for our present and future. It's a shame you never truly understood me. Now I feel truly cheated." Tears continued to flow freely.

Outside the room, the situation in the hall and outside the villa was becoming increasingly loud and tense as more people joined the crying.

"When did this happen?" "Did the news reach them?" "Sad" were some of the many phrases echoing through the house.

That didn't bother Adi and Nidhi, who were in their own world, just a room away from the hall.

"Stop it, will you?" Nidhi snapped back, her voice louder, her anger a tempest. "Now you're making me the culprit, huh? This is how you treat someone who has trusted you and given you their life? To someone who all she wanted was love, you give neglect in return? Wake up, Adi. We're in a situation we can't get out of. But understand this and let's separate."

"Everyone has their own way of loving, Nidhi. Yours is expressive. Mine was too once, but it transformed into responsibility, care, and ambition for a better life for both of us. But love and affection are all there. It's a pity you never saw that in these seven years. The truth is, even now, at this bitter moment of l...i...f...e, whatever you're talking about separation, I'm still thinking about staying together."

"Whatever, Adi! This will go on. Okay, do you want to miss the commotion outside? Let's go see what's happening and settle our scores in the meantime."

As Adi and Nidhi entered the hall, pushing past the crowd, they reached the front gate where more than a hundred people were gathered around a white van. Some cars followed the van, and many people were walking behind it. Adi and Nidhi joined the walkers.

"It feels like ages since I've walked in this hot sun," Nidhi said loudly, her voice carrying to Adi.

"Knowing that, I bought your dream car, a pink Beetle, the first one on the market," Adi added slowly, raising his hands to shade her from the sun.

Pushing his hands away, Nidhi sighed, "Now what's the use? God, I miss my Beetle."

"Remember our first movie together?" Adi asked, his voice filled with a wistful nostalgia. "Yes, of course! 'Janemann,' while I was waiting to watch 'DON,' which released the same day. Oh god, one thing after you came into my life, you got me into Salman Khan. After that, my heart always had space for you, my first crush Shah Rukh, and Salman," Nidhi added with a naughty smile.

Adi mocked in a typical Shah Rukh Khan style, "And you made me, the hardcore Salman fan, a Shah Rukh fan. 'Jab Tak Hai Jaan,' you made me watch it 10 times in PVR."

"Now, we're both going to miss watching 'Chennai Express' on the first day," they both said at the same time, their laughter a bittersweet melody.

The van entered a large ground, and everyone waited around it for the two bodies to be brought out, covered in white cloth. Adi and Nidhi stood near the van, their hearts heavy with anticipation.

Four people slowly carried the two bodies out and towards the pyre, followed by everyone else. As they placed the bodies on the pyre, Adi pointed to one of them, his voice trembling, "Look at that, you're just like a sleeping baby."

Nidhi pointed to the other, her eyes filled with tears, "So are you!"

As the pyre was set on fire by an elderly man with tears in his eyes, performing the last rituals, Nidhi came closer and held Adi's hand, her grip tight, "Adi, this is the most difficult phase of anyone's life. To witness their last journey. To see their beautiful bodies, which we've taken care of for years, now being burned and charred by fire into ashes."

Adi hugged her tightly, his body trembling, "Sorry for everything, darling. I may have cheated you and hurt you badly. Now you're completely free to go and live your life. I can't stop you anymore."

Nidhi held him tightly, kissing his lips, her tears mingling with his, "Idiot, where are you going? We didn't expect this twist so early in our lives. Otherwise, we would have been really busy our entire life – fighting, arguing, making love on the balcony, having a baby, naming her, growing her, and then fighting again. That's okay. Despite that, one good thing happened is, you have all the time in the world for me. I can fulfill my wish list with you."

"Coffee in Milan, lovemaking in French wine yards, long drives on the Nevada highway, or the first day, first show of 'Chennai Express,' the moment is ours. Let's not waste it."

As the most beautiful and loving souls left their burning bodies in the Aryan Cemetery, Mumbai, leaving behind their dismayed and sad parents and friends in gloom, they faded into the smoke spreading around, ready for another dream.

"Death struck the most beautiful couple of Rishi Villas, Colaba West this morning, Adi and Nidhi Kemkar, a young couple who were on their way to the temple to celebrate their 8th marriage anniversary. They were hit by a lorry while trying to save a girl from getting hit by their car. Death happened instantly as the lorry ran over their small car. The heartbreaking fact is that they died holding hands," Channel 9 dedicated a sweet farewell to this sweet couple. "Goodbye Adi and Nidhi, with condolences from Channel 9 and everyone with a heart." The news reporter concluded her coverage outside the cemetery gate.

Love prevails!

THE LUCKY LOAF

"The villagers looked up at the sky with hope, their eyes fixed on the dried well that had been lifeless for six months. Suddenly, a bolt of lightning struck the sky, and everyone closed their eyes. When they opened them, the well was full of water, and the barren land had transformed into a lush, green expanse. Trees bore fruit all around. Tears of joy streamed down the faces of the villagers as their days of starvation were over, and the deaths in their families due to hunger would no longer be a threat. Their prayers had been heard."

As I wrote the final line of my story, I saved it in a document and closed my laptop. A sense of satisfaction filled my heart, but my stomach rumbled with hunger. I left my workspace and went to the kitchen to disturb my mom. As always, she was busy. Being quite orthodox, my mom never let me enter the kitchen without taking a bath. Today was no different. Her eyes said it all: "Do NOT ENTER."

I shouted, "Breakfast!" and she replied, "Shower."

The heavy clanking of metal and shouting from outside diverted my attention, and I went to the balcony to check what was happening. My father joined me, reading his newspaper. "There's a big wedding happening. Big celebrations," he said.

I was puzzled. "Who's getting married?"

"The daughter of Lucky Kuber, the owner of this Sun Shine Gated Community, and not only this one, but fifty others like it in the city. The real estate tycoon, the one with assets worth 2500 crores and counting, Mr. Karan Bedi's one and only daughter is getting married here tonight."

"I still don't understand why such a rich man would choose to have his daughter's wedding here," I said.

"That's a good question, son! Because when he first ventured into this business, this was his first venture, and after that, there was no stopping him. He considers this place a lucky mascot for him."

I left the balcony and sat on my bed, listening to my dad's interesting discussion. "Not only that, there will be a gala for the next three days here, with continental cuisines by the world's best chefs, music and entertainment by Bollywood performers. The guest list includes all the who's who of the city. And that's not all, there will be a special performance for the couple by Bollywood superstar S Khan tomorrow evening. Son, he's spending 200 crores on this wedding. Can you imagine?" My dad continued talking, but my mind was lost in thought.

"Stinking rich people waste money on their luxurious lives, while the poor struggle to survive. This fat seth doesn't have any heart for the slums around, which he has occupied to build these luxurious villas in the city. He's dancing on their throats with pride." With a mix of anger and frustration, I stood up to go for a shower and then to the office.

My mom came to my room and shared the news with surprise. "Son, do you know this? Mr. Bedi is sending two large family pizzas to every family in the community as a gesture and, of course, we're all invited for the evening dinner. Don't be late."

"Two family pizzas to 400 families?!," I laughed to myself. "With that money, we can feed 100 hungry souls for a week." My mind was racing with calculations.

The door knocked five minutes later. My dad and mom looked at me as if I were the designated door opener in our house.

There stood a pizza delivery boy holding two pizza boxes in his hand and a beaming smile on his face. I returned a genuine smile. He said, "Good morning, sir. Complimentary from Mr. Bedi, two family pizzas for our sweet home, sir. Enjoy!"

I thanked him, took the boxes from his hands, and placed them on the table before closing the door. The pizza delivery boy was still standing there, his smile unwavering.

I asked him, "What is it?"

"Sir, Mr. Bedi has organized a lucky contest for every family in this community. To participate, you have to take a piece of your pizza, put it in this packet, write your name and flat number on it, and give it back to me. Mr. Bedi will pick the lucky loaf, and the family who gave it will be rewarded with 50,000/- worth of free coupons to Pizza Den. And that's not all, 3 lakhs worth of gold for that family."

My ears perked up at the mention of the contest. Initially, I thought it was a ridiculous idea, but when he said "3 lakhs," my ears started ringing with the sound of gold.

I turned back and looked at my parents, and I could tell they were going through the same thoughts.

Without much hesitation, I took a piece of pizza, put it in the packet, wrote my mother's name and flat number on it, and gave it back to the delivery boy. I asked him, "When will the results be announced?"

He simply smiled and said, "By tomorrow morning, the news of the lucky loaf will be shared with the entire world. All the best." He left without turning back.

As I left my flat for the office, I overheard people talking about the lucky loaf that could win a family 3 lakhs worth of gold.

"Guru is in the right house during this time. In fact, my astrologer told me I would be getting unexpected property this week," I overheard the community secretary saying. I laughed at his statement and left in my car.

As my car passed through a slum near our place, I saw a family of four living in a house made of gunny bags over a drain. I wondered what 3,00,000/- would mean to them. Would it be life-changing?

As the day went on, this entire episode faded into the background as my boss, deadlines, and new assignments occupied my mind. In the evening, my mom called me to share the news (or rather, rumor) that the Coimbatore aunt who stays on our floor claims she has won the gift and is spreading the news everywhere. I didn't react much, knowing her reputation as the "Rumor Express."

A late evening meeting with a client made me reach home at 12, and of course, my mom greeted me with anger for missing dinner.

I slipped into my room, saying, "Don't worry, mom, you have to give me a nice dinner party tomorrow evening if you win the gold tomorrow."

My mom's early morning prayers woke me up without the need for an alarm the next day. The moment I woke up, I checked for my dad to find out who the lucky winner was.

My dad handed me today's newspaper and pointed to an article on the main page, with photos. The photos showed a hundred children sitting on the floor, looking into the cameras with thin, frail smiles. They looked more like skeletons than children, with no life in their eyes. Yet, through those lifeless eyes, I spotted a smile of gratitude. My heart sank at the sight of the children's plight, but as I read each word of the news, my heart filled with ultimate happiness and bliss.

More than 300 children of Arunoday Balashram, the city's oldest orphanage, had been facing severe hardship for the last few days due to the death of the founder and trustee, Shri TG Rao, a freedom fighter. No one had come to take responsibility, and the government had delayed the takeover for three months.

Things had worsened ten days ago when the food resources ran out, leaving the children and staff struggling to manage even one meal a day. In the past week, even that had become impossible. The staff had resorted to begging for food, and many children had to survive on water. Yesterday, three children had died of starvation, and five more were in critical condition.

Then, the magic loaves from the 400 benevolent residents of Sun Shine Gated Community had saved the children's lives. The loaves of pizza, filled with love from each flat, had provided sustenance to these innocent children. The government had sent food resources by evening, ensuring a life-saving dinner for the 300+ children.

The news article thanked the kind residents of Sunshine for their generous act.

As I folded the newspaper, tears of happiness streamed down my face. I noticed the same in my dad's eyes.

"Those who did this must have God within them," my dad said.

Was it Mr. Bedi who did this? Or the pizza delivery boys? Whoever it was, the kindness within them had listened to some of our prayers and given the lucky loaf to those who truly needed it, those who were more deserving of the 3 lakhs worth of gold that everyone was greedily waiting for.

Unlike in my stories, God didn't need to perform magic to show his existence or reassure the humans in trouble. His impact, his magic, his presence was felt among us through these tiny yet powerful acts

AN ENCOUNTER WITH GOD!

Tonight will be a grand gala for the gods, for sure. For the first time, all the gods on Earth are meeting for an awards ceremony, competing in various categories – Best God, Popular God, Most Popular God, and more.

Journalists like me and fans of their respective gods are waiting on either side of the red carpet, their eyes filled with enthusiasm. We're eager to witness the gods walking the red carpet, waving to us. And when I talk about gods, I mean THE Gods, the fathers of this universe, the gods who created us and labeled us Hindus, Muslims, Christians, and so on. After thousands of centuries and eras of creation, it seems the time has come for them to decide who is greatest.

Hence, this countless years of contests and tonight's awards declaration ceremony!

What a day!

I wish the god I pray to every day, whom my family considers the deity, would be the winner. The BEST God!

But deep down, before being tagged as a Hindu, Muslim, or Christian, something tells me I'm a human!

A powerful race among all the creations of the gods. Hence, I've always asked myself these questions, before being convinced by the so-called societal norms of religion, god definitions, and their limitations.

Three questions always swirl in my mind, seeking answers. I believe I can get those answers from none other than my god. Fortunately, as a journalist for the ever-running magazine "World Humanity Digest," my god has granted me five minutes of his time.

My eyes are fixed on him. Oh God! There he is, my god, approaching me. I wave at him, and he waves back, coming towards me and taking me to a nearby seating area. Dressed casually, my god's style statement is truly godly.

As he relaxes on the sofa, closes his eyes, and speaks in a low yet powerful voice, he says, "You have three questions to ask me, and your opportunity starts now!"

It should be time that starts, right? Hmm, gods are timeless and ageless. Hence, time is not a factor for them.

Pausing to consider my countless thoughts, I asked my first question.

"Dear Mr. God, my first question: If you say birth and death are part of a cycle, why don't you ensure uniformity in that? Why are some people born in a castle and others in a slum? Why do many people die ghastly deaths, in accidents, suicides, homicides, genocides, natural disasters, and terror attacks? Why this disparity?"

He started laughing and said, "You called that a question? You asked so many questions in one! Funny, you humans!"

"Okay, here's the secret," he leaned down a little towards me and asked me to listen closely.

"You think heaven and hell are different worlds, set in some space outside your world? You're wrong. They're both around you and nowhere else, and especially here," he pointed to my head.

"It starts here and ends here. Your deeds or actions determine your fate. Quite a cycle we're stuck in," I answered myself.

Before I could ask my second question, God interrupted, "Dude, I already answered your second question. Now jump to the final one."

There goes my God! What a genius he is! He read my mind and sensed my next question about heaven and hell.

Or rather, what a fool I am to consider God a genius!

"God, my final question goes like this. You exist in various forms/ avatars across religions throughout time and have been a different god to every religion out there in the world. But tell me something, are there many gods in the world of ants, rats, or elephants?"

"Do cats fight among themselves in the name of different gods?"

"Does the caste difference prevail among pigeons?"

"Are there untouchables in the world of fish?"

God couldn't stop laughing, and I looked at him like a puzzled fool, which I was.

God finally regained his composure and said, "The only defect that happened in your creation was that you were born with a tumor in your head, and the tumor is called the brain. Its symptoms are quite destructive. While one part of it makes you the most powerful race in this universe, the same cells provoke you to destroy yourselves completely."

"The same tumor made you so insecure with each other that you created an illusory hypothesis, the power that guided you to lead life in this world has given you a special message – The World is all yours. Love each other.

Unfortunately, you humans have taken the first sentence so seriously that you've formed human gangs and named them religions, created your own forms of me as your gods, and waged war against other religion gangs.

The war is continuing and will go on! The truth is, the war is happening in your own minds."

"God, forgive me! I always believed in the truth you've revealed now. But why do I see different gods out there when you say there's only one?"

God stood up and started walking away from me. He stopped at a certain distance, turned back, and looked at me deep into my eyes. "Close your eyes, free your mind. You've been looking at this world with those limited, senseless eyes. Now look with your soul eyes, free yourself from this body, and look at me. Tell yourself what you see."

I did as he said, freed myself from my senses and my mind, and opened my eyes. I looked at him with a question-free soul.

"God, you look like me! And what the heaven! All those gods who are walking around, they look like me!"

I am the God? Yes, I am.

A sense of overwhelming satisfaction filled my soul, and joyful tears streamed down my face. The answers lay within me. When I have no qualms, no limitations, no inhibitions, no feelings – I am the God!

Dear brothers, just break free from your Hindu, Muslim, and Christian tags and check this out.

THE WORLD IS ALL YOURS. LOVE EACH OTHER.

EVIL GOD WITH A SCARRED FACE!

My encounter with God provided answers about life and food for thought. I am God – that's the feeling I get when I close my eyes, free my soul from my body, and enter a thought-free world. It's an unimaginable feeling, a phase of pure bliss. But beyond this godly state, a dark shadow lurks, waiting to consume me. I'm confused and feeling helpless.

Am I losing this magic suddenly? What's happening? Is my godly feeling not forever? What is this feeling that's taking over me? Pride? Arrogance? A feeling of dominance? What is it?

I woke up from my bed and looked into the mirror. I could see myself, but I couldn't see myself. I mean, I could witness my eyes, nose, and other body parts, but something had overtaken me.

"Seems like my brother has started influencing you too!" A voice sounded eerily similar to mine. I looked around.

"Look at me, here, you fool! Last time, you waited to see me and yourself in me, and this time you can't recognize yourself."

Oh, yeah! God had stepped into my room, and I hadn't noticed.

"Hi," I said with a positive smile on my face. He didn't notice me and was busy looking at himself in a new avatar. Finally, he stood up and started walking around the room. Wearing a long robe, he looked very different today.

As I watched him, awe-struck, he suddenly drew a weapon from his robe. My eyes widened in fear as I saw a large gun, reminiscent of those used in the MIB (Men in Black) movie. Big and deadly looking, the gun was beyond my comprehension.

AK 57, 58, 59, 60, 61... my mind raced, counting numbers as fear coursed through my veins. I tightly closed my eyes, waiting for the moment of death to come as the God slowly pointed the gun at my face.

As I was about to urinate in my pants from fear, God laughed loudly, put away the gun, and settled back on the sofa. "Fear is the ultimate weapon in this universe," he said. "The more you invest in it, the more control you have over this world."

The phrase sounded intriguing but came from the wrong source. Why on earth would God say this? Where were the blissful words that usually came from the mouth of this omnipotent, omnipresent, and omniscient God?

Thoughts raced through my mind before I could open my mouth and ask my question.

The so-called God before me said, "Yeah, yeah, I know what you're thinking. Simple... I'm also a God, or rather, I'll make you believe me. Just that my brother always rules the bright side, and I take the dark side. And I always rule."

Evil... Devil... Satan... my mind started spelling out those names for this God of darkness. Surprisingly, he looked similar to my god. Or rather, they were alike, until they revealed themselves.

He came closer and looked into my eyes, saying, "We both are within you, in an inexplicable mix – God and Satan – GodSatan mix. This mix is life."

His words were as influential as my God's, even more sweet and attractive!

Before he could say anything else, I closed my eyes, took a step back towards the wall, and pressed my body against it. I took a deep breath and felt a warmth on my hands.

I opened my eyes and looked at my God, now dressed in a cool Gucci outfit. With a simple smile on his face, he said, "This is my brother to you, who rules this world as much as I do. For ages, we've been fighting. He always dominates, but in the end, I triumph, and the war continues.

This war happens within every one of you, in that tumor of yours. Good vs Bad, Selfish vs Selfless, these wars are far more frightening than the nuclear wars happening outside your world. Because those bio wars are the result of my brother's triumph in your mind.

If you lose belief in yourself, Evil triumphs. If you hold belief in yourself, I am always the winner. Believe in good, believe in benevolence."

I closed my eyes again. I didn't know what to believe in now. God or Satan. But one thing was clear: they both existed within me.

Good exists, so does Bad, and that's what makes me human. The difference lies in which one prevails. If God prevails, it makes me a superior human being or even a god. If evil prevails, it turns me into a ferocious devil.

Everything is true, but being godly is the ultimate truth that saves the planet from any doomsday.

Bring in the God and spit out the evil!

Pavan Kumar Parimi, often calling himself a "dream engineer" and a lifelong learner, brings over 15 years of expertise in marketing, branding, and advertising across diverse industries. Known for his dreamer persona, Pavan's creative flair shines through his campaigns, many of which have challenged conventional norms. A true Scorpio, his intensity and passion fuel everything from his work to his wanderlust. An avid traveler and adventure motor cycling enthusiast, he finds inspiration on the open road. Pavan is also a die-hard movie buff. Based out of Hyderabad, he's now turning his storytelling passion into authorship with his debut novel, *Bahuvidha.* With a sharp wit and an eye for detail, Pavan's writing gravitates towards historic fiction and the intricacies of human relationships. And if there's one thing he knows for sure, that a well-crafted story is like a good adventure—unexpected, thrilling, and always unforgettable.

www.ingramcontent.com/pod-product-compliance
Lightning Source LLC
LaVergne TN
LVHW091328150826
845673LV00006B/1801

* 9 7 9 8 8 9 5 5 6 9 7 7 1 *